Seduction

By Velvet

The Black Door
Seduction
Betrayal
Naughty

Seduction

A Black Door Novel

Velvet

PAN BOOKS

First published 2007 by St Martin's Press, New York

This edition published 2013 by Pan Books
an imprint of Pan Macmillan, a division of Macmillan Publishers Limited
Pan Macmillan, 20 New Wharf Road, London N1 9RR
Basingstoke and Oxford
Associated companies throughout the world
www.panmacmillan.com

ISBN 978-1-4472-3162-2

1 3 5 7 9 8 6 4 2

A CIP catalogue record for this book is available from
the British Library.

Printed and bound by CPI Group (UK) Ltd, Croydon, CR0 4YY

Visit **www.panmacmillan.com** to read more about all our books
and to buy them. You will also find features, author interviews and
news of any author events, and you can sign up for e-newsletters
so that you're always first to hear about our new releases.

To my Dad, now I have my very own personal Angel watching over me! Rest peacefully. I love you even in the next life!

acknowledgments

Seduction was a joint effort, and these amazing people were instrumental every step of the way:

Everyone at St. Martin's Griffin—my dynamite editor, Monique Patterson; Matthew Shear; John Murphy; Abbye Simkowitz; Kia DuPree; and all those who had a hand in making *Seduction* a reality.

William A. Boyd, Jr.—Bill, you are the bomb photographer, thank you for sharing your talent with me! Denise Milloy, once again your makeup skills transformed me into a star! Saundra Warren and Crystal Roach, thanks for taming my mane. I'm so glad you're both a part of my Glam Squad; now I have no Glam-O-Rama Trauma!

Sara Camilli, I am so blessed to have you as my agent; thanks for all of your hard work over the years!

Thanks to my loving family and fabulous friends whose love and support are invaluable; you know who you are! And a special shout out to Ron Shipmon, Kenneth McClure of Hospitality Holdings, Jeff Pogash of Moët Hennessy, Hue Man Books, and the Pleasure Chest for helping to make the New York book signing party for *The Black Door* a huge success!

And a huge thank-you to the readers who enjoy my Black Door stories!

Much Love,

1

BUSINESS AT the Black Door, New York's only adult playground exclusively designed for women, was thriving. Owner Trey Curtis had conceived the concept one night while at Scores—a high-end strip club—as he watched men and *women* take pleasure in scantily clad dancers, disrobing and gyrating onstage. While the men were forthright with their wants and desires, some of the women seemed a bit reserved. Trey sensed that the ladies didn't want to be judged by prying eyes, and that's when the idea for the Black Door was born. Shortly thereafter, he opened a women's only club where members could partake in as many carnal activities as they could handle. And to ensure anonymity, so that they could really feel sexy and uninhibited, he personally designed identity-concealing masks. The only men allowed to enter the Black Door were servers, hired to entertain and please members with anything from a stimulating conversation to a stimulating orgasm.

The Black Door was housed in a three-story brownstone located uptown in the Washington Heights area of Manhattan. Trey spared no expense in decorating the club; he imported gold-leaf wallpaper from Italy for the foyer and installed an eight-tier crystal chandelier to give the entrance a regal appearance. He wanted the members to feel like pampered queens the moment they stepped across the threshold. And to accomplish that goal there were two parlors on the ground floor where members could mingle, have cocktails, and loosen up before venturing upstairs.

In one of the parlors, hidden behind a crimson velvet drape, was a narrow staircase that served as the entry to the second level. Upstairs, along a dimly lit corridor, which seemed to stretch for blocks, were a series of doors that led to various chambers where the serious activities took place. Trey exhausted his imagination when he created the various theme rooms. There was the Voyeurism Room, where through a one-way mirror members could watch one another get their brains fucked out. In the 8mm Room, vintage porn flicks played nonstop for those who needed a little visual stimulation to get the juices flowing. The Pink Room was geared toward members who wanted some girl-on-girl action; everything in the room was pink from the lighting to the drinks to the furniture to the exposed pink pussies. The club even had its own bar. The Leopard Lounge was inviting, with black and tan leopard print walls and private booths, so members could relax while sipping on the club's signature martini—the Black Door—made of Moët & Chandon White Star and a splash of Hennessy.

The club was sexy yet sophisticated, and had something for everyone's comfort level, which made it popular among the ladies who fucked around on the side. So popular in fact that Trey had to open a second club. Overseeing the operations of the Black Door took up the majority of his time, and whatever was left of the day was spent dealing with his personal problems. He had a few unresolved issues from his past that kept him preoccupied. Though Trey loved running the club, he knew that he couldn't handle both clubs successfully, so he hired Mason Anthony to manage the Black Door Two.

Mason Anthony had risen through the ranks from server to escort—which was another component of the business—to manager. Mason wasn't keen on being a sex slave, because some of the women had insatiable appetites and could cum for hours, so he transferred over to the escort department. The escorts were under no obligation to maintain a rock-hard cock; they accompanied clients to black-tie banquets, award ceremonies, parties, and private dinners. Mason was the ideal date-for-hire; he was a towering six feet four inches, with well-defined triceps, biceps, and deltoids. Even his gluteus maximus was firm and looked great in a pair of slacks. His cocoa brown skin matched his sensuous brown eyes to a tee, and his black goatee framed a pair of full, kissable lips. The icing on Mason's cake was his sexy Denzel-like strut. When a client strolled into an event with him on her arm, she was sure to be the envy of the night. Not only was he handsome, he was articulate as well.

Mason had only worked as an escort part-time while he attended med school, but when his funds ran out and the grants dried up, he approached his boss about returning to the club as a server (since they made more moola), but Trey had something else in mind. He needed someone whom he could trust to run the Black Door Two, and Mason fit the bill perfectly, since he knew all aspects of the business. When Trey offered Mason the job as manager, he eagerly accepted. The opportunity meant a chance for him to stack his cash so that he could return to school and become a surgeon. In addition to a generous salary, the job also came with generous perks—like being in the company of beautiful women 24/7— which he enjoyed immensely. Mason hadn't been in a committed relationship in eons, so on those lonely nights when he got horny, he donned his bronze mask and prowled the club for a willing victim.

Since all the members and servers were screened for STDs, Mason could fuck without fear of catching some kind of dreaded disease.

The Black Door Two was located in an old warehouse in the trendy Meat-Packing District, an area of the city that had been gentrified from bloody meat-packing storehouses into multimillion-dollar lofts, pricey boutiques, and hip bistros. From the outside, the six-storied brown brick building looked abandoned, and that's exactly the look that Trey was going for when he bought the property. Unlike most of the buildings in the area that had been totally gut-renovated, Trey chose to keep the exterior untouched so as not to cause any unwanted attention. He kept the four bottom levels in their original condition, but rehabbed the top two floors. If you didn't know the club existed, you'd assume that this was just another old dilapidated warehouse. There wasn't even an address on the building; the only discerning mark was a black metal door. Unlike the uptown club that serviced a more mature clientele, the downtown location catered to the Generation Nexters; young trophy wives who were tired of spreading their legs for potbellied husbands who popped Viagra like Tic Tacs in order to get a woody; and well-bred East Side debutantes who put their sweater sets aside and slipped into see-through lingerie for an evening of uninhibited freakiness.

"Evening, Boss," the elevator attendant greeted Mason.

"Hey, Moe, how's business tonight?" Mason wanted to know. Moe was the keeper of the gate, and since no one could enter without riding up in the freight elevator, he kept a mental count of how many members entered the club.

"Business is good." He smiled slyly.

Mason knew exactly what Moe's smile meant. It meant that he had seen more than his fair share of tits and ass. Most of the members came to the club draped in capes, pashminas, and trench coats to conceal their outrageous outfits; but the moment they entered the elevator, those coverings were peeled off posthaste, revealing lace, leather, and little else.

Moe clanged the metal gate door shut, shifted a long, arm-length lever to the right, and the ancient elevator slowly began to rise. Once they reached the fifth floor, Mason stepped out. The club occupied the top two levels of the building. The oval entryway was painted pitch-black with silver flecks adding a reflective element underneath the glow of the overhead pin lights.

"What's up, Gee?" Mason asked the greeter. Gee was a huge hunk of a man, with steroid-enhanced muscles that made Mason's physique pale in comparison.

"Just hanging out enjoying my job." Gee grinned, wiggling his fingers in the air. He had the best J.O.B. in town. Gee was responsible for digitally stimulating the clients and getting their pussies all wet and juicy before they strolled into the inner sanctum of the club. Wearing only a light sheen of baby oil on his upper body, which enhanced his muscle tone, a camouflage mask and matching G-string, he was the perfect tweaker, and the women loved his touch.

Mason shook his head. "I'll just bet you do." He strapped on his bronze leather mask and walked toward one of the many doors that lined the perimeter of the entry.

The fifteen-thousand-square-foot loft was divided into several suites. In addition to the titillating theme rooms that were in the original club, the downtown location had a few special chambers of its own. There was the Naked Pool Room, where members played the game in the buff wearing only their identity-concealing masks and pumps. In the Mani/Pedi Spa, women got toe- and finger-sucking manicures and pedicures. And in the Chocolate Chamber, buffed servers smeared liquid chocolate all over members' breasts and clits, and then licked off every inch of the decadent sweet. The Disco was a throwback to Studio 57, the seventies nightclub where celebrities, models, and a smattering of lay people were among the select few who partied underneath a mirrored disco ball until the sun rose, set, and rose again.

Mason could hear the pulsating beat of Donna Summer belting out "Love to Love You Baby" as he made his way to the Disco. He had a stack of paperwork a mile high sitting on his desk, but he decided to peruse the club before heading upstairs to his private office. Mason was love-starved, and needed to take the edge off before he could concentrate on work, and a little eye candy was the perfect solution. Once inside, he stood back in the cut and scanned the room. The dance floor was packed with masked women and servers dressed in provocative outfits. He had seen more sheer negligees than Frederick's of Hollywood, so the see-through numbers were doing nothing for his libido tonight.

Just as Mason was about to leave, in walked a short, curvaceous woman wearing a red plaid micro-miniskirt, black platform boots, a teeny-tiny midriff sweater, and a white mask. He watched as she grooved her way to the center of the dance floor. The crowd parted slightly as she began to gyrate to the beat. Her skirt was so short that Mason could see her butt cheeks wiggle with each move.

"Now that's what I'm talking about," he whispered to himself.

Once her ass was in motion, she began moving her shoulders quickly, causing her extra large jugs to jiggle. Mason could feel his groin heating up as he watched her titties bounce up and down, and the way they shook freely, it was apparent that she wasn't wearing a bra. He licked his full lips as he watched her shake her groove thang. She spun around in a circle, causing her tiny skirt and long dark hair to spin in the breeze. She was seducing him with her fluid dance moves, and as much as he was trying to restrain himself, his dick was growing harder and harder. He had come into the Disco to watch, but now with a serious hard-on between his legs, he wanted to do more than just observe from a distance. As Mason abandoned his position in the back of the club and strolled onto the dance floor, he was no longer thinking with his brain, because his dick had taken over.

Her back was turned and she didn't see him as he slipped up behind her and placed his hands on her hips. She turned her head slightly to see who was dancing with her, and when she saw the bottom half of Mason's handsome face, she smiled and turned back around.

That smile was all Mason needed. He knew that it was his stamp of approval to do whatever he wanted, and he wanted to fuck. As he seductively swayed back and forth with her, he slid one hand down to her thigh and underneath her skirt. She wasn't wearing any underwear, not even a thong, and the feel of her smooth ass made his dick grow an inch. He reached down farther until he was touching her pussy lips.

"Oh, yeah, Papi," she moaned in a heavy Latin accent, and leaned forward so that he could have easier access.

Mason looked around to see if they were the only ones on the dance floor getting jiggy with it, but everywhere his eyes turned, people were fucking and sucking. Everyone seemed caught up in their own world and oblivious to their surroundings. He removed his other hand from her waist, unzipped his jeans, and flipped out his cock. He rubbed his massive member in between her cheeks until it was as hard as slate.

"Fuck me now, Papi," she demanded.

Her commanding voice turned him on and he slowly entered the head of his dick into her ready pussy, doggy style. Once inside, he grabbed her hips and firmly pulled her toward him.

She bucked him back. "Fuck me harder. Fuck me harder!" she panted.

Mason couldn't believe that someone so small could take all ten inches of his rod, but she was giving as good as she got, so he rammed her pussy repeatedly as hard as he could until they were both dripping in salty sweat.

"That's it, Papi! Give me all of that dick."

He grabbed her around her tiny waist and nearly lifted her off the floor with each thrust. Mason could feel himself cumming, so he pulled out and shot his load on the back of her sweater, and the fuzzy material quickly absorbed the creamy substance, leaving a wet mark in the center of her back.

The second he released his grip from around her waist, she flipped down her skirt and danced away as if nothing had happened. Mason put his dick back in his pants and made his way through the crowd and out the door.

Once inside his office, he went into the bathroom and washed up. He took his mask off and looked into the mirror.

"You gotta stop fucking around with the clients," he told himself, his brain now returning.

Though Mason could indulge anytime he wanted, he knew that it was unprofessional and distracting. Besides, he was tired of just "fucking," and wanted a real relationship, something he hadn't had in years. But ever since the Black Door Two opened, his libido was on high alert, and he'd been using the club as his personal playground. Sex at the club was addicting and he couldn't seem to satisfy his insatiable appetite; it was almost as if he were possessed by a sex-crazed spirit. He knew what he needed to curb his extracurricular activities was a monogamous relationship. A relationship with a hot sexy intelligent woman would keep his mind off the random women he encountered nightly. He wasn't commitment phobic like some men and enjoyed the companionship that a relationship offered. However, he was having trouble finding Ms. Right. He knew that she was out there somewhere, but the question was . . . where?

2

SAGE HIRSCHFIELD was the heir apparent to the media empire that his grandfather had built some sixty years ago. Hirschfield Publishing was one of the nation's biggest media conglomerates with newspaper, magazine, and book publishing holdings. Since his graduation from grad school, Sage had been a junior executive under his father's watchful eye. After six years of tutelage, the elder Hirschfield was finally ready to step aside and relinquish the reins to his son. Sage could have easily sat back, rested on the company's laurels, and ran the day-to-day operations without making any major changes to the well-oiled machine. But he wanted to put his own imprint on the organization, so with his father's blessings he bought a bankrupt movie studio in the hopes of turning it around by producing quality films.

At twenty-nine, Sage was one of Manhattan's most powerful business moguls and had the world at his fingertips. Strikingly handsome, he was a true mutt, since his bloodline was mixed with four different ethnicities. His grandfather, a Jewish immigrant from Russia, married a half Italian, half Native American woman, and they had two children, one of whom was Sage's dad, Henry. In college, Henry met and fell in love with Lisa Jones, a black girl from Brooklyn. Sage's look was a combination of his colorful heritage. His coal black, curly hair was in stark contrast to his bright latte complexion, and his prominent nose was a blend of Jewish, Indian, and African. With his exotic looks, Sage would get asked all the time, "What are you?" And to that he would answer, "Black." Though he wasn't trying to deny his ancestry, he believed that the mother's race defined the child's, and his mother was a beautiful black woman—whom he loved dearly—so as far as he (and society) was concerned, he was black, even though he looked half white and had a Jewish surname.

Mega-rich, with a megawatt smile, Sage had done his stint as an international playboy. He'd dated supermodels in Milan, Paris, and New York; starlets in Hollywood and Bollywood; and a couple of Olympic athletes from Norway and Poland. His wild escapades were so notorious that he graced the gossip pages of tabloids around the globe. With his playa days behind him, Sage was ready to settle down and get married, and there was only one woman who fit his criteria—Terra Benson.

An heiress to the Benson and Viceroy Tobacco Company, Terra had been the girl of his dreams ever since they were kids. Their fathers were friends and belonged to the same country club, so Terra and Sage had known each other since childhood. A couple of years older, he had seen her grow from an awkward teen into a beautifully poised woman. Terra possessed the qualities that any man would want; she was smart, classy, beautiful, and rich—so rich in fact that he didn't have to worry about her gold digging for his fortune. The only problem was that Terra thought of him as just a friend. She made it clear on several occasions that he was "like a brother." It irked him to no end when she referred to him as family. Sage already had two sisters and didn't need a third. He'd done everything in his power to win her over, from sending exquisite Mikimoto pearls to candlelight dinners at four-star restaurants, but nothing seemed to faze her. Little did she know that her aloofness only made him want her more. Sage was a man of results, and he made a solemn vow that he would win Terra over, no matter what.

"Mr. Hirschfield, Ms. Walker is on line one," his assistant announced over the intercom.

Missy Walker was Sage's fuck du jour. Even though he loved the soles of Terra's designer shoes, he was a man with needs and Missy satisfied those needs to perfection. By night, she was a professional stripper, but by day, she was his "Girl 6," and called most afternoons for their phone sex ritual.

"Thanks, Pearl," he said, clicking over. "Hey, Baby, how's my kitty cat doing?" he asked, getting right to the point.

"Wet and ready," she purred like Eartha Kitt into the receiver.

Sage licked his lips at the thought. "Put your fingers in that ass and tell me how tight you are."

"Oh, Daddy, it's as tight as a drum," she told him.

"I want you to reach underneath your legs and stick your middle finger in that tight hole," he instructed.

"And I want you to take that big dick out and stroke it for me," she whispered seductively.

Before unloosening his Hermès belt buckle, Sage got up and locked his office door for added privacy. He unzipped his pants, sat back down, and reached inside for his joystick. The head of his dick was already swollen from the sound of her voice, and his cock was throbbing. He opened his desk drawer, took out a tube of K-Y jelly, squirted a glob of the clear gel into his hand, and rubbed it over his aching dick. He jerked his shaft up and down, and up and down, and up and down until he was ready to explode. "Oh, Baby, Daddy's cumming!"

"Wait, Daddy, let me put my mouth on that big cock of yours, so you can cum in my mouth. I wanna swallow that hot load."

"Yeah . . ." he panted, "suck up all of Daddy's cum, you dirty little whore!" The visual of him feeding Missy a mouthful of his cum made him even hornier.

"Give it to me, Daddy. You know I'm a greedy slut who needs all of that creamy cum. Now stroke that dick harder."

"Ohhh," was all he could manage to say.

"Harder, harder, stroke it harder," she hissed into the receiver.

He masturbated faster and faster until a stream of cum shot out onto his pants and dripped down on his shoes. "Missy, you know just how to make my day," he said after composing himself.

"Same time tomorrow?" she asked.

"You'd better believe it." He smiled into the phone. He did and said things to Missy that he would never utter to Terra. He couldn't imagine calling Terra a whore or a slut; she was much too refined for dirty talk.

After Sage hung up, he walked into his private bathroom, took a quick shower, and changed clothes. He was a metrosexual, and made it his business to stay well groomed. He kept an armoire filled with an entire wardrobe of tailored shirts, suits, designer ties, shoes, and underwear.

He looked in the mirror and tied his lavender silk Michael Newell tie into a thick Windsor knot. He was taking Terra to Chanterelle for dinner and the restaurant required gentlemen to wear a jacket and tie, not that he wouldn't have dressed appropriately anyway. Sage slapped his cheeks with Creed, put on his custom-designed navy suit jacket, and headed out the door.

"I'm off, Pearl. I'll be on the cell if any urgent calls come in," he told his assistant.

"Okay, Mr. Hirschfield. Have a good evening."

Sage had planned on having a spectacular evening. He had

gotten his rocks off, now he was going to see Terra, the love of his life. He hadn't seen her since her graduation from Yale a few months ago. Now that she was finished with college and living back in the city, he planned on seeing a lot more of her. He knew that Terra considered him family, but with time he was confident that he could win her heart. He had patience and that was indeed a virtue. Besides, he had Missy to soothe his blue balls until he won Terra over.

3

"SO WHAT time is your dinner over?" asked Lexington, Terra's best friend.

"I should be done around nine-thirty at the latest." Terra didn't really want to go to dinner with Sage, but he had insisted on taking her to the four-star restaurant for a belated graduation celebration, so she couldn't say no.

"Cool. Should I pick you up at the restaurant?"

"No!" Terra sounded alarmed. "I don't want Sage asking me a bunch of questions, so you better pick me up at the apartment."

"Okay, see you around ten-thirty; that way it'll give you time to change from your dinner suit into your—"

Terra cut her off, "Don't even say it!"

"Yeah, all right." Lexington chuckled and hung up.

Lexington and Terra had been best friends since kindergarten; they were Jack & Jill alumni—the ultra bougie children's club for affluent African Americans—and spent their summers together in the Hamptons on the shores of Sag Harbor. If there was one person in the world who knew Terra inside and out, it was Lexington. Like an old, worn-out journal, Terra confided her innermost secrets to her best friend, and Lexington did the same. Terra carried herself like a dignified debutante, wearing white button-down shirts with cashmere sweaters tied around her shoulders and crisp jeans in the daytime and couture St. John suits in the evening. From her outward appearance, most people assumed that she was a "good" girl, but Lexington knew better. Like a true Gemini, Terra definitely had two sides to her personality; one side was reserved, while the other side was Wild, with a capital "W."

Tonight, Terra was having dinner with Sage Hirschfield, a childhood friend. She had known Sage since birth, and thought of him as a brother. Over the years, Terra noticed that he had developed a crush on her. And it was becoming more and more apparent, because every time he invited her to dinner, the restaurants were romantic and befitting of a couple in love, not a couple of childhood friends. Terra thought that he was handsome but wasn't interested in him romantically. In her mind's eye, he was still a skinny boy in ill-fitting clothes and wire-framed glasses.

Terra showered and decided to wear a midnight blue, vintage Chanel suit, the pearls Sage had given her as a graduation present, and a pair of matching pumps. She pinned her long hair up into a French twist and let a few pieces hang loose to frame her face. She spritzed each side of her neck with L'Heure Magique, a delicious scent by Laura Mercier. The scent was subtle yet sexy, just like her. Once her look was complete, she walked back into her closet and took out an outfit for the second half of the night. Unlike her conservative dinner suit, this ensemble was anything but conservative. She carried the pieces over to the bed and laid them out on the duvet. Terra looked down at the clothes and smiled slyly; she couldn't wait to shed her suit and slip into her other life, but first she had to get through dinner.

Terra's two-toned silver Maybach was waiting outside of her Riverside Drive apartment; she loved being chauffeured around the city, especially during rush hour when it was difficult to find a taxi. The car and driver was a graduation gift from her father, as well as the comfy two-bedroom condo with expanding views of the Hudson River and the George Washington Bridge in the distance. The driver immediately hopped out and opened the passenger door the instant he saw her approach the car.

"Good evening, Ms. Benson," he said, tipping the bib of his black driver's cap.

"Hello, Leroy."

"And where are we off to tonight?" he asked once she was settled into the plush leather backseat.

"Chanterelle, 2 Harrison at the corner of Hudson," she told him.

As the car cruised down the West Side Highway, she peered out of the tinted windows and marveled at the view. She could clearly see New Jersey across the river to her right and the sparkling city lights to her left. New York was so full of life and it felt good to be a resident of Manhattan. She had grown up in Old Westbury, one of Long Island's posh communities, and though she made regular trips into the city, it didn't compare to actually living there.

The traffic was light, and within fifteen minutes they were pulling up in front of the restaurant. Located in a beautifully restored alabaster stone building, Chanterelle was an exclusive four-star restaurant. Intimate in scale, with exquisite overhead chandeliers and tables set with crisp white linen tablecloths, bone china, crystal, and silver, Chanterelle was usually the destination of choice for momentous occasions for many New Yorkers.

Terra waited in the backseat until the driver came around and opened the door. He reached inside and held her hand to help her out (not that she needed any assistance, but it was protocol and expected).

"Thanks, Leroy. You can pick me up at nine-thirty." Terra knew that she would be rushing dinner, but she didn't plan on lingering over coffee and dessert. The night was young and she had other plans for the rest of evening that didn't include Sage.

"Okay, Ms. Benson, I'll be here." He smiled.

The moment she entered the cozy foyer, Sage swept her up into a tight hug. "Hey, Gorgeous."

Terra was caught off guard and nearly lost her balance. "Hey there," she said, trying to free herself from his clutches.

He released her and scanned her from head to toe. "You look good, Girl!" He grinned.

"And you're not looking too bad yourself." She had to admit that Sage was *GQ* handsome and could have easily graced the pages of the glossy magazine.

"Flattery will get you everywhere." He winked.

"Sir, your table is ready," the hostess interrupted, and escorted them into the well-appointed dining room to their choice table near the back.

Within seconds, a server appeared and asked for their pre-dinner cocktail preference.

"We'll have a bottle of Veuve Clicquot Grand Dame," Sage told him.

"Champagne?" Terra asked once the waiter disappeared. "What's the occasion?"

"Anytime I get to have dinner with you is a special occasion," he gushed like a schoolboy. "Plus, I haven't seen you since your graduation, so this is a celebration," he said, searching for a reason to wine and dine her.

Terra knew that it was just an excuse, but she played along anyway. "That's so sweet of you, Sage. I couldn't ask for a better play brother," she said, jabbing him in the arm. "And thanks again for the Mikimotos"—she touched her neck—"they're beautiful."

Sage cringed slightly. The last thing he wanted to be was her "play brother," or any other brother. He wanted to be her man, and somehow he had to convince her that they were made for each other. "No problem, I'm glad you like them. I hope you're hungry. They have a wonderful tasting menu that I think you'll enjoy," he said, ignoring her brotherly comment.

The last thing Terra wanted was the tasting menu; it was at least six courses and would take longer than an hour and a half. If it were her choice, she would have ordered an entrée sans appetizer, so she could be on her merry way. "Sounds good," she lied.

The waiter came back with a chilled bottle of champagne and two crystal flutes. After pouring, he began his spiel. "Tonight's tasting menu is divine. We start off with Chesapeake Bay Crab Cake drizzled with Almond Oil, followed by a Wild Mushroom Risotto sautéed with Foie Gras. And for entrées, we have Grilled White Tuna with Watercress Coulis and Loin of Lamb with Fresh Mint, and an assortment of Artisanal Cheeses will be served before dessert. We also have a tasting of New and Old World wines to complement the meal."

Terra had to admit that the food did sound delectable, so she would just bite the bullet and enjoy each course.

"So what are your big plans now that you've graduated?" Sage asked, once he had ordered for them both.

"Well, I plan to make good use of my theater degree. I've already found an agent and have been out on go-sees."

Sage looked surprised. "I didn't know you majored in theater. I just assumed you were a business major and would join your father at his company."

"You mean like you did?" she said condescendingly.

"Don't make it sound like a bad thing. I actually enjoy working in the family business."

"What's there to enjoy? Your grandfather and father laid all the groundwork, so what's there for you to do except follow in their footsteps and collect a check?"

"That would be true if I were the type to sit back and take credit for their accomplishments, but I'm not. As a matter of fact, I just bought a movie studio and am starting Hirschfield Multimedia, a subsidiary of Hirschfield Publishing. So you see, my dear, there's quite a bit for me to enjoy," he said, setting the record straight.

At the mention of "movie studio," Terra instantly perked up. She hated going on those cattle calls, grouped with all the other wannabe actresses. "Wow, that's awesome," she said with a grin. "Maybe now I won't have to pound the pavement," she said with an air of relief.

Sage squeezed his eyebrows together in confusion. "What do you mean by that?"

"What I mean is . . . now that you're a big-time movie mogul I don't have to go on those stupid cattle calls. You can just cast me in your films," she said naïvely, solving her own career dilemma.

Sage didn't know what to say. There was no way he was going to mix business with his personal life. That was the first rule his father taught him; he'd said that was the fastest way to lose a friend—business and friendship didn't mix. And the last thing Sage wanted was to lose Terra's friendship. But watching her sitting there looking excited and doe-eyed, he couldn't tell her flat out no, so he just said, "We'll see."

Suddenly Sage began to look better in her eyes. If she had to cuddle up with him to become a star in his films, then she would. Terra knew that he wanted her in the worst way, and all it would take would be for her to show him a few skills that she learned in college. Except the skills she had in mind didn't come from any class, but she had to play her cards just right. Sage was savvy and wouldn't take kindly to being used, so from this moment on, Terra would begin the process of converting their relationship from friends into lovers.

4

LEXINGTON SAMUELS, by all accounts, was *the* ultimate party girl. She came from family money, so she didn't have to log in eight hours a day at some boring J.O.B., like the mass majority, which gave her plenty of time to paint the town in varying shades of red. The family made their fortune when her mother took an old family recipe and began making maple syrup from her kitchen. After years of dedication and perfecting the technique, a major food corporation bought the recipe and licensed the name "Samuels Homemade Syrup," making Lexington and her parents millionaires. And to ensure that the money would last several generations, her father invested in dotcom stocks before the technology market went belly up. He made gobs of money from his investments, then flipped the profits and invested in real estate. He bought dilapidated buildings in Harlem and Brooklyn, waited for the neighborhoods to turn around, and then gut-renovated the properties and sold most of them for four times what he'd paid. He kept a few buildings as rental properties.

At her parents' insistence, Lexington went to NYU and majored in journalism, but she had no intention of becoming a journalist or working for a living for that matter. The only reason she had agreed to go to college was the location of the campus. New York University was in Greenwich Village, one of the city's most popular areas filled with cool clubs, college bars, and cute cafés. Lexington wasted no time getting acquainted with all that the Village had to offer. She spent more time hanging out than she did in class, and during her freshman year she nearly flunked out. Her parents threatened to pull her out of NYU and enroll her in an all girls college upstate if she didn't get her act together. With the fear of being banished to the country and surrounded by nothing but women and woods, Lexington reprioritized and began attending class regularly. To her parents' delight, she graduated in the top ten percent of her class, but their joy was short-lived when she turned down an offer to work as a staff writer for *The Post*. Lexington read "Page Six" of *The Post* on a daily basis, but she was more interested in being written about in the gossip pages than writing the pages herself. Unlike her best friend, Terra, who shied away from the flash of the paparazzi, Lexington lived for press coverage. It made her feel like a celebrity. The only problem was that she wasn't famous or rich enough to garner coverage on her own, so she relied on Terra for exposure. Terra Benson was the heiress to the Benson Tobacco Company; her family's money was old and long, much like the Hiltons'. And like the young Hilton heiresses who dominated the tabloids, the press loved to track Terra's comings and goings, and when they did photograph her—which was rare—Lexington was right by her side glamming it up.

Lexington had been waiting impatiently in the lobby of Terra's building for over forty minutes and she was getting antsy. They were going to the opening of a new hotel and Lexington wanted to get there before the press left. "Finally," she huffed once Terra came rushing through the revolving doors. "Where the hell have you been?"

"I'm so sorry, Lexi." Terra gave her a quick peck on the cheek. "But Sage insisted that we have the tasting menu, and you know how long and drawn out those courses are."

On the elevator ride up to Terra's apartment, she told Lexington all about Sage's plans to start a movie studio.

"So, do you really think he's going to let you star in his films?" Lexington asked skeptically. She also knew Sage from childhood, and knew how conservative his family was when it came to business. On one occasion, her father approached his father about partnering in a business venture, but the senior Hirschfield told him in no uncertain terms that he didn't believe in mixing friendship with business, and if Sage was anything like his old man, he probably thought the same way.

"Well, he didn't exactly say no."

"But he didn't exactly say yes either, did he?" Lexington asked.

"No he didn't, but I plan to slowly wrap my charms around him until I have him under my spell and then he'll do anything I want," she said confidently, as she opened the door.

Lexington chuckled. "You sound like David Copperfield and David Blaine rolled into one."

"Just call me Ms. Magic and watch me work it out." She held up her hand for Lexington to slap her five.

Lexington greeted her hand with a smack and then said, "Okay, Ms. Magic, why don't you use your skills and make a quick transformation, because we're running late."

"Ha, ha, very funny. Pour us a drink while I change; there's a bottle of Veuve in the fridge."

Terra went into the bedroom to make her transformation from

debutante to diva. She took off her tailored blazer, unzipped the
A-line skirt and let it fall to the floor; then she removed the nude-
colored panty hose. Once she was free from the confining conservative suit, Terra pulled on a pair of Chip & Pepper "Walk of Shame"
ultra low-rise jeans and a rhinestone-trimmed, black wife-beater.
She removed the bobby pins that held her long hair in a French
twist and let it flow freely down her back. To complete her club
look, she slipped her feet into a pair of Giuseppe Zanotti sandals
with rhinestone toe straps. After tousling her wavy hair (for that
messy unconstructed look), Terra powdered her face and applied a
coat of Bobbi Brown nude gloss to her lips.

"That's what I'm talking about," Lexington said, commenting
on her outfit once Terra walked out of the bedroom. "Now you look
like you're ready to hang with me instead of with my mother."

"Girl, you know I have an image to maintain. My parents
would flip out if they saw me dressed in low-rider jeans down to
my crack. They think I'm their little princess and that's exactly
what I want them to think. Until I land that million-dollar role, I
have to keep the peace so the money'll keep flowing."

"I hear you, but my folks know it's no use trying to tame me, so
they finally stopped trying to," Lexington said, taking a sip of
champagne.

"Aren't you afraid they'll cut you off financially?" Terra asked
worriedly. She couldn't imagine not having the financial support of
her family. She'd lived in the lap of luxury all of her life and she
wasn't about to give up her six-hundred-dollar shoes, fifteen-
hundred-dollar purses, and two-hundred-dollar lunches, so if she
had to put on a front until she could properly support herself, then
she surely would.

"No, they're cool. Besides, it's not like I have a quarter-of-
a-billion-dollar inheritance to worry about like you do." She handed

Terra a flute of champagne. "Come on, drink up so we can go," she said, changing the subject.

Before leaving, Terra put on a pair of dark, oversized shades to help conceal her identity. Even if her picture was snapped tonight, she wouldn't be recognizable as Terra Benson the heiress, because the photographers would be looking for a French-twist-wearing, conservatively dressed young woman, not a wild-haired, tight-jean-wearing hussy. She'd crafted her uptight image to such perfection that nobody would believe that she was capable of blending into the club scene.

To keep her secret life secret, Terra had given her driver the rest of the night off. She didn't want him driving her around from club to club just in case he reported her whereabouts directly to her father (after all the driver was on her father's payroll). They hailed a taxi in front of Terra's building and headed downtown.

Their destination was the opening of the NoLiTa Grand, a swanky boutique hotel north of Little Italy. Once filled with low-rise tenements, the area was now thriving with local designer boutiques; Cuban, Spanish, and French restaurants; a smattering of clubs; and now an ultra-sleek hotel. The private party was being held to christen the lower lounge of the hotel as the next New York hot spot.

From half a block away, Terra could see flashbulbs popping at the entrance to the hotel. "Maybe I shouldn't go in," she said nervously as the cab inched its way forward.

Lexington gave her a "you must be kidding" look. "Why? What's up?"

"There are too many photographers out front, and I don't want to wind up on *Page Six*," she said, fidgeting with her Chloe clutch.

"Take a chill pill, T. Even if they do snap your picture, they'll never associate you with being Terra Benson, so you can relax because you look nothing like your normally boring self," Lexington reassured her.

Terra took the compact out of her purse and checked her image. She fussed with her hair, making sure it covered a good portion of her face; with the huge glasses and wild hair, she felt confident that no one would recognize her. "Okay; you're right. I hardly know myself," she said with a renewed sense of confidence.

To Lexington's disappointment and Terra's joy, they made it through the throng of reporters and photographers without anyone asking for an interview or snapping a picture. To the press, they were invisible, just two random chicks trying to hang with the celebrities. Little did the paparazzi know that they had just missed the scoop of the evening by not recognizing the wealthy young heiress.

Terra's nerves subsided once they were inside. The lounge was packed shoulder to shoulder with downtown hipsters—artists, models, actors, and designers—grooving to the funky beats of the DJ Mista Ish and sipping bubbly. The event was being sponsored by Moët & Chandon, so the champagne was flowing freely. Terra and Lexington wasted no time getting two flutes from a passing waiter, and with their drinks in hand, they prowled the scene looking for cute guys to flirt with.

"Now he's fine," Lexington said, discreetly nodding in the direction of a tall, buffed man with overgrown pecs, a slim waist, and a tight ass. She smiled in his direction, but her smile quickly faded when another man approached him.

"Yeah, and so is his boyfriend," Terra said, watching the two men snuggle up together.

"What's with these *Brokeback* dudes?" Lexington asked, rolling her eyes to the ceiling. "It never fails; every time I'm attracted to a good-looking man, he's either gay or bisexual."

"Gay I can understand, but those bisexual in the closet guys are scary. I mean they have wives and girlfriends, but have sex with their 'boys' on the side, all the while saying that they're not gay. Well, if being poked in the ass ain't gay, I don't know what is," Terra said, slightly hunching her shoulders.

"The ones that are doing the pitching don't consider themselves gay, because they're doing the fucking and are not being fucked."

"Pitching or receiving, it's all gay to me." Terra shook her head in disgust. "I can deal with a lot of issues, but being bisexual isn't one of them. In my book, either you're straight or you're gay. I can't stand those guys who like to double dip. It's just so nasty." She drained the last of her drink. "Let's change the subject, because this one is too depressing."

"To all the *Brokeback* men, let 'em stay in the mountains." Lexington raised her glass in a mock toast.

The friends drank to straight men and continued prowling the VIP area in the hopes of finding not one but two available men.

5

"MAN, YOU'RE doing an excellent job managing BD Two. The month-end numbers have far exceeded expectation, and it's due to your vision of adding the new theme rooms," Trey told Mason as he sat in Mason's office on the sixth floor of the club.

"Thanks, Man." Mason smiled as his boss showered him with praise.

"This club is so popular that we now have a waiting list for new members. Who would have thought that the younger women would be so into this type of scene?" Trey asked.

"There are a ton of young horny women who married older men for money and status, only to find their husbands can't get it up without that little blue pill. So the chicks come here to get their freak on with our servers who don't need over-the-counter help to stay hard." Mason leaned back in his chair and put his hands behind his head, relishing the moment. He had worked hard to make the Black Door Two a success and now all of his efforts—hiring a hot young DJ, inventing new theme rooms, and promoting the club through steamy Web sites—were paying off. "Now that I think about it, we should raise the initiation fee for new members. These spoiled rich chicks can more than afford to pay to play." He laughed, but was dead serious.

"That's a brilliant idea! Mason, you're a lifesaver. Between running the Black Door and dealing with my personal life, there would be no way on earth I could've handled running this club too." Trey sighed heavily.

Mason leaned forward. "Speaking of your personal life, how are things going with you and Michele?" he asked, knowing the history between Trey and his overly possessive girlfriend.

"They're going fine for her. She lives in Washington during the week, working for my dad, and—"

"Trey, I know I've said this at least a hundred times since your dad won the nomination last year, but I'm so proud of him. I'm so proud, you'd think that he was my father."

"Yeah, I'm proud of him too. He worked his entire life to get to the Supreme Court, and to think he almost lost everything because of me."

When the nominating senator discovered that Trey owned the Black Door, he immediately took Preston's (Trey's father) name off of the short list of qualified candidates, claiming that he was guilty by association and the press would crucify him once they got wind of Trey's ownership of the scandalous club.

"But he got everything back because of you. Don't forget that major detail," Mason reminded him.

Once Trey realized that his father was being denied the opportunity to throw his hat in the ring, he called Senator Oglesby and politely informed him that if he didn't put Preston's name back on the list, then he would have no other choice but to inform the press about Mrs. Oglesby's extracurricular activities. Not only was the senator's wife a card-carrying member of the Black Door, she had also been fucking Mason on the side. The senator nearly collapsed from shock and embarrassment. After he recovered, he quickly reinstated Preston's name, and used his powerful connections to keep Preston from being associated with the Black Door. The rest, as they say, is history.

Though Trey had told Mason about jeopardizing his father's chances of sitting on the Supreme Court, he hadn't told him about unknowingly sleeping with Ariel, his father's wife—well, she hadn't been Preston's wife at the time—because he still felt guilty about betraying his dad. They had met at the Black Door, when Ariel came to the club wearing her best friend's mask. He had no idea who she was; the only thing he knew was that they shared an intense chemistry. Their passion was magnetic and they couldn't keep their hands off of each other. They fucked randomly at the club a few times, until his mask fell off one night during their heated lovemaking. The second Ariel saw his face she ran out on him. Fortunately, the situation was working fine for the time being, except now Trey had an unwanted girlfriend. Michele—whom he met through his dad—refused to accept the fact that they were mismatched. The only thing that they had in common was sex, and once the sheets cooled off, they argued nonstop. Trey had been trying to break off their relationship for a long time, but she wouldn't hear of it. Michele knew about Trey's affair with Ariel, and whenever he talked about breaking up, she threatened to tell his father about his deception, but she hadn't said anything yet. So until he could figure out a way of protecting his dad from the truth, he'd have to deal with Michele's unwanted affection in order to keep her mouth shut.

"Things are going well for her, but what about you? Are you happy?" Mason asked, with concern in his voice.

Trey dropped his head, hesitated a moment, then looked up at Mason and said, "Happiness is a luxury I can't afford right now."

Hearing the melancholy tone in his voice, Mason said, "Come on, let's go down to the club. I think you could use a momentary diversion to cheer you up."

Mason walked over to his private closet, took out his bronze mask, and handed Trey a plain black mask that he kept on hand in the event one of his boys dropped by and wanted to check out the club.

They took the private staircase that led from Mason's office to the club's entry. "Hey, Gee, what's up?" Mason asked the club's greeter.

"Man, it's hot up in here tonight." He shook his hand at the wrist for emphasis. "A group of chicks from the East Side just came in *Looking for Mr. Goodbar*." He chuckled. Gee knew from experience that the East Side women came to the club wearing Burberry trench coats in varying colors on the outside, but the same tan and black plaid lining on the inside. They carried designer purses that cost more than his used two-door Jeep, and they had an air of entitlement—as if the expensive trinkets that they wore entitled them to snub anyone out of their über-rich league. But once they crossed the threshold of BD2, and the coats came off, they were as raunchy and wild as the rest of the members, if not more so.

"Which way did they go?" Trey asked. He'd been in a monogamous relationship longer than he cared to admit. His record for being faithful was usually thirty days, but he'd exceeded that record by nearly a year. Getting caught with his hand in his father's cookie jar was enough to scare him into monogamy, but now that the dust had settled, Trey was ready to sample a few tasty treats.

"I think they went into the Naked Pool Room," Gee told him.

"Come on, man. Let's check out their game." Mason winked.

A periwinkle felt-covered pool table sat underneath a silver dome light and was the focal point of the room. Instead of a bright white bulb, the light emanating from the dome was periwinkle as well, giving the room a dim, seductive glow. Mason and Trey stood in the doorway and watched two teams of blondes battle each other in a game of Eight Ball.

One woman, who looked to be at least six feet tall, had one knee on the table while her other long leg rested comfortably against the side of the table. When she leaned into her shot, she lifted her leg off of the floor and pointed it into the air. Balancing herself on only one knee, she looked like an erotic dancer. Despite her orchestrated efforts, she missed the cue ball by a mile.

"It's our game now," said a blonde wearing a pink corset, which was tied so tight that it pushed her boobs together, causing them to nearly spill out.

Trey could see her pink areolas, which matched her mask and corset perfectly. His eyes were glued to her as she bent over at the waist and aimed her cue stick. She leaned over so far that one tittie popped out. He licked his lips as he watched her nipple brush against the surface of the table. She hit the cue ball with such force that her other tittie sprang loose. The white ball hit its intended target and she jumped up and down as the orange ball dropped into the upper left pocket. Trey could feel his dick spring to life as he watched her full breasts bounce up and down.

"Game!" She grinned and slapped her partner high five.

"We got next," Trey announced.

The women turned in the direction of Mason and Trey, and when they saw the two handsome hunks, all four of them smiled. "What are the stakes?" asked the winner.

"We'll make it easy on you." Mason grinned. "If we lose, my partner and I will gladly suck your pussies until you come. And if we win, you'll get on your knees and buff the helmet."

"We wanna play too," whined the blonde from the losing team.

Mason smiled at Trey because he knew that within minutes they would be getting their dicks sucked by four blond bombshells. "The more the merrier." He grinned.

They let the women break first, and they sank a solid ball, but on their second turn they scratched, sinking the cue ball into the lower right-hand pocket. Mason went next. He hit the green-striped ball, which ricocheted off of the red-striped ball, causing both balls to drop in simultaneously. Mason was on a roll, banking and pocketing balls right and left. He felt like Minnesota Fats (minus the fat), as he wielded his cue stick, sinking all of their striped balls. With only the eight ball standing between them and an evening of fellatio, Mason called his shot, concentrated, aimed, and sank the black ball with one smooth hit of the cue stick. He turned to Trey and gave him a high five.

"Man, I didn't know you had game like that," Trey commented.

Mason smiled slyly. "I learned my way around the pool hall in college. After being on the losing end too many times, I decided to take some lessons to improve my game," he admitted.

"That's not fair; you guys are pros," whined the same blonde who wanted to be included in the game.

"If it'll make you feel any better, I'll suck your clit as a consolation prize," Mason offered.

"Now you're talking," she said, and hopped on top of the pool table.

Mason walked over to her, spread her legs apart, and patted her pussycat. He then took his hand and pulled down her thong. He fingered the petals of her pussy, and began to play with her pink clit.

"Hmm," she moaned at his touch.

He could feel her getting wetter with each stroke. His mouth began to salivate in anticipation of tasting her sweet juices. He teased her a little longer before traveling south. He pushed her back on the table, threw her leg over his shoulder, and began feasting.

While Mason had his head buried between the legs of one

blonde, Trey was on the other end of the table with a trio of blondes. One woman was on her knees sucking his dick, while another licked his balls. The third woman played with her nipples while watching and waiting her turn to wrap her lips around his big black dick.

Trey reveled in all the attention that he was getting; it was just what he needed to take his mind off of his problems. These women were servicing him so well that he forgot all about the fucked up predicament that he was in with Michele. Mason was right; a little excitement was exactly what he needed to escape, even if it was just for the moment.

6

FEODORA KONDRASHCHENKO, known as "FK," was also known as "The Barracuda" (behind her back of course). FK was the fiercest talent agent in the business. Her parents were Russian Holocaust survivors and had instilled in their daughter the will to not only survive, but to thrive by any means necessary. Feodora's father, Saul, founded the talent agency after coming to New York and witnessing all the young people fighting for auditions on Broadway. He saw an opportunity, hung up a shingle, and opened shop. Feodora worked alongside him and learned the ins and outs of the business, and when Saul retired, she took over as CEO and ran the business with an iron fist.

"What do you mean I can't get my hands on a copy of the script?" she screamed into the receiver. Feodora was on the telephone with Fred, an associate in her West Coast office.

"I spoke to the head of development over at Warner, and he

said that this project is wrapped so tight that no one will be allowed an advance copy of the script," Fred informed her.

"Did you tell him it's for me?" Feodora was not used to hearing the word "no." She was relentless and refused to take no for an answer.

"FK, I told him, but he still said 'no.' "

She fumed at the two-letter word. "Don't worry about it. I'll just have to go over his head. I have someone in mind as the lead, and I want to read over the script before every agency in town has a copy."

"Sorry, FK, but I tried," Fred apologized and hung up.

"He's got to go," Feodora said to herself. Fred had been with the company for a year, and during that time he'd yet to step up to the plate and deliver the goods. She'd given him ample time to grow, but he was a slow learner, and slowness was something she had no tolerance for. Feodora made a note to call HR regarding his termination and then dialed one of her favorite clients.

"Hello?" Terra answered the phone in a groggy voice.

"Don't tell me you're still in bed?" Feodora rose before dawn every day, and had put in a full day's work before noon. She was the type of person who only required four to five hours of sleep per night, and didn't understand those people who needed eight hours of beauty rest.

Terra looked at the clock on her nightstand. "It's only nine-thirty." She sighed.

"And you should be up reading the trades," Feodora chided her. By nine-thirty, Feodora had read every industry publication on the planet, and even managed to comb through the *New York Times,* *The Wall Street Journal*, and the *Los Angeles Times.* "If you're serious about the business, you have to stay abreast of what's happening before it's old news," she said, continuing her scolding.

Terra silently mouthed, *Whatever.* Even though she loved her agent, she didn't love being talked to like a three-year-old. Terra flipped the covers off of her body and strode to the front door. She had all the entertainment trade publications delivered right to her door every morning. Usually she was up by eight o'clock, and by nine-thirty had finished every single rag, but this morning she was still a little hungover from the night before. She and Lexington had gone to another hotel opening and had stayed out way past three in the morning. "Calm down, FK. I've got all the papers right here in my arms, and they will be read before the clock strikes noon." She chuckled, trying to lighten the mood. "Anyway, I'm sure you didn't call to harass me about reading the trades."

"I have an audition for you tomorrow at two-thirty. It's for a Dove commercial. They're looking for the All American Beauty to launch their new facial beauty bar. And I think you'd be perfect to represent the new line."

This time Terra mouthed, *I don't think so.* She wasn't interested in auditioning for some damn television commercial. She wanted to be a movie star, and though she knew some actresses started their careers doing commercials, and then branching off to act in soap operas before making it big, she had no interest in either. Now that Sage was buying a movie studio, she could forgo the "paying your dues" part of the business and start right at the top. "No thanks, FK. I think I'll pass."

Hearing that two-letter word again nearly sent Feodora over the edge. "What do you mean, *no thanks?* At this stage of your career, which may I remind you is at the beginning, you can't afford to turn anything down but your collar. If I send you out on a hundred go-sees a day, you should be happy," she hissed into the receiver.

Sensing that she had pissed off Feodora, Terra began to explain. "Wait a minute, FK, don't think I'm not grateful for all you've done. It's just that I found out the other night that a good friend of mine is buying a studio, and he has agreed to let me star in his first film." Terra knew she was stretching the truth, but she had to do some damage control so she wouldn't lose her agent.

Feodora was privy to most of the insider information in New York and Hollywood, but she hadn't heard anything about a new studio cropping up on the scene. "Who's your friend, and what's the name of the studio?"

"His name is Sage Hirschfield and he's starting Hirschfield Multimedia," she said, beaming through the phone.

"Sage Hirschfield?" Feodora knew of the Hirschfields. They were one of the most powerful families in the publishing industry, but she hadn't heard anything about them buying a movie studio. As she sat there and thought about their branching off into film, it made perfect sense. The Hirschfields had conquered publishing; now, obviously, they planned to do the same thing in the entertainment industry.

Hearing the inquisitive tone in Feodora's voice, Terra clarified their relationship. "We grew up together." She smiled into the receiver and added proudly, "Our families go way back."

Even though Feodora treated Terra like any other starving actress, she knew that Terra was far from hungry. She was a Benson with money *and* connections. Having her on the client roster was beneficial to Feodora, even if Terra wasn't the most talented actress in the stable. And after learning about the new Hirschfield acquisition, Feodora knew that she had made the right decision by accepting the young heiress as a client. "Hmm, I see. Well, let me make a few calls and find out exactly where they are in the process, but in the meantime, I want you to go to the audition, *and* don't forget to read today's trades," Feodora instructed, refusing to take no for an answer.

Realizing it was useless arguing with FK, Terra relented and said, "Okay, I'll be there."

After Terra hung up, she showered and slipped on a pair of snug low-rider jeans, a stark white Thomas Pink shirt, and a pair of black Gucci loafers. She stuffed the trades into her Hermès tote, threw a cashmere cardigan around her shoulders, and headed out the door. Terra was hooked on the Chai latte at Borders. It was like liquid crack, and she couldn't seem to get enough of the delicious tea concoction. Fortunately, there was a Borders around the corner from her apartment.

She hurried into the bookstore to get her daily dose of the sugary blend, but everyone on the West Side had the same idea, because the café line was ten deep. Terra noticed that there were only two available tables, so instead of waiting in line, she made a beeline to the only window table left, pulled out the trades, and set them square in the middle of the table. She took off her sweater and placed it on the back of the chair. After staking her territory, she stood in the long line with the rest of the junkies and waited to get her fix.

With a large cup of Chai latte in hand, Terra settled in at her table and began pouring over the trades. An hour later, she had finished reading half of the publications and was in the middle of *Variety* when a voice asked, "Excuse me, is this seat taken?"

Terra looked up, and standing in front of her was a gorgeous-looking man with a body straight out of *Men's Fitness* magazine, and a handsome cocoa brown face straight out of *GQ*. He wore a tattered Brooklyn Dodgers T-shirt and a pair of gray jogging pants. White iPod earphones were wedged in his ears, but he obviously didn't have the music turned up, because he stood there, looking at her, waiting for an answer.

"No, it's empty," she said, and continued reading. Though he was as fine as a runway model, Terra had no interest in striking up a conversation. She was on a mission, and that mission entailed persuading Sage to let her star in his first production. Terra was determined to be an actress, and she didn't want to be distracted by a relationship. The only man she was interested in sexing up was Sage, because he held the key that could unlock the door to stardom.

Mason had just come from a run along Riverside Drive. He'd recently moved into the neighborhood and loved jogging along the Hudson. It was serene along the water, and the cool breeze off the river allowed him to clear his head before beginning a long night at the club. He had planned to get his double espresso to go, head home, take a shower, and get ready for work, but the moment he saw her sitting there looking like the epitome of the perfect woman, he couldn't resist himself. She sat near the window, and the bright, midmorning sun highlighted her wavy, auburn hair. Her golden reddish tresses cascaded around her shoulders, framing her warm honey complexion, and made her stand out from the crowd. She was dressed casually, yet chic at the same time. The way she sat with her back as straight as an arrow and her legs crossed, Mason assumed that she had had some type of etiquette training. There was something unique about her and he wanted to know what made her tick, but before he could strike up a conversation, she pulled out her cell and made a call.

"Hello. Terra calling for Sage," she said in a no-nonsense voice.

Ahh, so her name is Terra, Mason thought, eavesdropping.

"Oh. Do you know what time he's expected back in the office? Well, just tell him that I called. He can reach me on the cell. Yes, he has the number," she said, and flipped her phone shut.

I wonder if she's calling her man? Mason thought. He looked at her left-hand ring finger and didn't see an engagement ring or wedding band. He smiled to himself, *Well, at least she isn't married. So whoever this Sage person is, he isn't her husband.* A boyfriend he could deal with, but he'd had his share of dating married women. He wanted his own woman, not some other man's wife.

Terra glanced across the table at him, and he appeared to be deep in thought. She came to Borders almost every morning, and hadn't seen him before. She thought about asking if he was new to the neighborhood, but changed her mind. She didn't want to give him the impression that she was interested, so she decided to leave before he initiated a conversation. She took one final sip of her latte, gathered her papers, stuffed them back into her tote bag, tied the sweater around her shoulders, and headed out the door.

Mason turned around in his chair and watched her sashay out of the bookstore café. She had a sexy strut, and though her blouse and sweater were conservative, her jeans hugged her ass suggestively. *I bet she's one of those "lady in the street and freak in the sheets" type of babe,* he thought. Mason had seen that type numerous times at the Black Door. He was intrigued not only by her looks, but also by the way she had snubbed him. Mason was used to women falling all over themselves to get his attention, but she had barely looked in his direction. He was a typical testosterone-driven male, and loved the thrill of the hunt, and from what he could tell, she was well worth the chase.

7

"OOO, BABY, that's it! That's it!" Missy moaned as Sage rammed his ten-inch rod deep into her ass from behind.

Sage had taken an early lunch and headed straight over to Missy's apartment in midtown. She lived within walking distance of his office, in a condo building on West Sixtieth Street. The one-bedroom corner unit was forty stories high, with floor-to-ceiling windows and spectacular south/west views of the city. Though the view was breathtaking, Missy couldn't see clearly because Sage had her face pressed so close to the glass that the river view to the west was skewed. "Take . . . all . . . of . . . this . . . big . . . dick . . . Bitch!" he breathed between each thrust.

Missy bucked back. "Give it to me, Daddy!"

Sage was on the verge of cumming but pulled out instead; he didn't want to cum just yet. Missy was a pro and he wanted to prove that he could go the distance, and not wimp out like an amateur.

He grabbed her by the waist and flipped her over, so that she sat on the edge of the windowsill.

"This afternoon is your treat," she purred, "so let *me* entertain *you*." She stood up so that he could sit on the windowsill instead, then dropped to her knees and began sucking his cock like it was a Slow Poke.

"Ooo, Baby, that feels sooo good," he moaned.

To intensify the sensation, she gently massaged his balls while deep-throating him. She was sucking, licking, and massaging at such a rapid pace that Sage nearly lost his balance.

He didn't want to lose control of the situation so he pulled her up by the elbows, turned her around, and lifted up her dress. He was so horny that he didn't bother taking off her thong; he just moved the thin strip of fabric to the side and eased his cock back into her anal passage. He slowly increased his pace until he was butt-fucking her so fast that her feet left the ground with each thrust.

"Ooooo, yesssss, Baby, that's it; that's it," she sang out in ecstasy.

"Take this dick, you dirty slut."

"Give it to me, you filthy bastard."

Sage slapped her ass and rammed her harder. "Is this what you want, Bitch?"

"Is that all you got, you fucking nasty ass fuck?"

"You like it rough, uh, Whore?"

"Yeah, Motherfucker, I like it rough. Now fuck me harder, you dirty bastard."

Sage was going out of his mind with lust and desire. He loved talking dirty, and Missy knew just what to say to drive him over the edge. He grabbed her by the titties and rammed his cock so far up her shit hole that he could feel his sperm-bloated balls slapping against her inner thighs. Sage felt his army of sperm on the verge of escaping, so he set them free and exploded deep within her ripe ass.

"Damn, Baby, you're the best," Missy purred, stroking his ego.

She knew Sage was the overachiever type, who loved to compete, so she told him just what he wanted to hear. Not that the sex wasn't good, but in her line of business, she had had better.

"Am I?" Sage asked, seeking another compliment.

"Oh, Baby, believe me, you definitely know how to work that big dick of yours. You had me cumming so many times I could hardly catch my breath," she said, laying the compliments on thick. Missy knew the fastest way to separate a man from his money was good sex, and giving him kudos on his prowess afterward.

Sage smiled proudly, as if he'd just won Olympic Gold. "I'd love to stay and give you more of this pole"—he grabbed his crotch for emphasis—"but I need to take a shower and get back to the office." He pulled her close, kissed her on the neck, and took a whiff of her perfume, which smelled sweet like fresh-cut flowers.

"There're clean towels on the counter, and a brand-new bottle of Molton Brown shower gel in the shower rack, and there's lotion on the counter." Sage was the ultimate metrosexual and loved expensive bath products, so Missy kept his favorite toiletries on hand.

Sage grabbed his clothes off the back of the sofa and went into the bathroom. Twenty minutes later he reemerged looking as fresh as a spring day. The tailored, dove gray suit hugged his shoulders ever so slightly, and the handmade, stark white shirt accentuated his pecs perfectly. His high-powered executive look was completed with a rose pink silk tie, tied in a thick Windsor knot.

"I left you a little something on the nightstand," Sage said, grabbing her close and giving her a deep French kiss.

Missy tongued him back. "Thanks, Baby. See you soon."

"I'll be tied up in meetings for the rest of the week and won't be able to break away, but I'll be sure to call you in case I need a little telephone loving." He winked.

"You can call me anytime," she said, opening the front door and letting him out.

Once Sage was gone, Missy went straight into the bedroom and looked on the nightstand. Lying near the telephone was a stack of bills. She picked up the cash and counted ten crisp one-hundred-dollar bills. She sniffed the money and fanned it across her face. Missy loved the smell of tax-free money more than she loved sex. Between stripping and entertaining private clients on the side, it would only be a matter of time before she could stop paying rent on a condo that didn't have her name on the deed and buy a place of her own—among other things.

"MR. HIRSCHFIELD, YOUR FATHER is waiting for you in your office," Pearl informed Sage the moment he stepped through the door.

"Really?" He wasn't expecting his father and wondered why he had dropped by unexpectedly without calling. "How long has he been waiting?"

Pearl looked at her watch. "About fifteen minutes." She picked up a stack of phone messages and handed them to him. "And Miss Benson called and asked for you to call her on her cell phone."

"Thanks, Pearl," Sage said, and walked into his office.

Henry Hirschfield was ensconced behind his former desk, talking on the telephone, as if he owned the place (in actuality he did!). "Marvin, I want to buy five thousand shares of Google at the market, and sell all of my shares of that Internet start-up company that I bought last week. I read in the *Journal* today that they just lost a major advertiser, so I'm sure their earnings will drop significantly before next quarter." Henry held up a finger and mouthed to his son, *Just a minute.*

Sage sat across from his dad and waited patiently. Sitting on the other side of the desk reminded him of all the years he had listened daily to his dad conduct business. It was during those early years when Sage learned firsthand how to wheel and deal. Even though he had a BA from Brown and an MBA from Harvard, Sage learned more from his father than from the prestigious Ivy League institutions. After six years of observing the master, Sage had been chomping at the bit and was ready to assume the role of chairman and CEO. He had yearned for the day when his father would retire, leaving him in charge of the company. When that day finally came, Sage comfortably moved behind the massive desk and began making a name for himself and not just relying on his father's past accomplishments. Now his sole goal was to take the company to another level and make his dad proud.

Henry hung up the phone and looked at his watch. It was almost a quarter to three. "Late lunch?"

"I had a meeting downtown with a writer friend of mine, and the traffic getting back to midtown was bumper-to-bumper," Sage lied. He had a meeting scheduled with the writer later in the week, so he just improvised on the dates. Having married right out of college, his father was the antithesis of a playboy. He'd been faithful to his wife from the first day they met, and couldn't fathom sleeping with another woman. Sage knew that his father wanted him to settle down and get married, and would strongly disapprove of him having casual sex with a stripper, so he kept the details of his afternoon to himself.

"Speaking of writers, how's the studio progressing?"

"I'm gutting the entire place and having new, state-of-the-art soundstages built. The renovations should take no longer than six months. In the meantime, I'm looking for material."

"Is this writer a good friend of yours?" Henry asked, looking suspicious.

"Actually, he's a friend of a friend, and has written a couple of novels and a few screenplays."

"Hmm, just remember what I told you about mixing business

with friends. Some people think they're entitled to special favors just because they know the boss. Don't get me wrong, I don't mind lending a helping hand, if the person is qualified and the best fit for the job."

"Not to worry, Dad, I would never hire someone on the strength of friendship alone. If there's one thing that I learned from you, it's that nepotism has no place here," Sage said, reassuring his father.

"That's good to hear, Son." Henry stood up to leave. "So, how's your love life?" he asked, catching Sage totally off guard.

"Uh, it's fine," he said, giving his father the short answer.

"Just fine?" Henry cocked his head to one side. "I'm surprised you haven't been snapped up yet. With your looks and position, the girls ought to be circling the wagons."

"Oh, trust me they're circling all right. I'm just picky, that's all."

"Well, I hope you pick someone soon. Your mother and I want some grandkids before we're too old to enjoy them." He grinned and patted his son on the back.

"Actually, I do have someone in mind." Sage smiled.

"Anyone I know?"

"As a matter of fact, you do." Sage hesitated a second.

"Well, don't keep me in suspense. Who is she?"

"Terra Benson."

Henry's face brightened up. "You mean little Terra?" Henry had always thought that Sage and Terra would one day make a dynamite couple. Since both families were rich and powerful, Sage wouldn't have to worry about some woman marrying him for his money.

"She's not so little anymore. We had dinner last week, and I must admit that she's grown into a fine young woman."

Henry's smile widened even bigger. "I'm so happy to hear that. Who knows, maybe there will be a wedding in the near future," he said, sounding like the hopeless romantic that he was.

"Slow down, Dad. Let's not rush things. Terra still thinks of me as her big brother."

"Just because you guys played in the same wading pool doesn't make you related," Henry said.

"Tell Terra that. I've tried making subtle overtures, but she's just not interested in dating me," Sage confessed.

"Just remember, Son, you're a Hirschfield and Hirschfields never give up the fight. So hang in there. I'm sure you'll win her heart before long."

"Thanks for the support, Dad." Since Sage didn't have any brothers, his father was his closest confidant. Aside from Sage's wild sex life, there was very little that he didn't share with his father.

"Keep me posted, and tell Terra hello the next time you speak with her. I hate to run, but I'm playing tennis at the club." He hugged his son and left the office.

Sage walked behind his desk, sat down, and dialed Terra's cell phone.

"Hey, you," she sang into the receiver.

"Hey yourself. You sound like you're in a good mood," Sage said, picking up on her happy tone.

"I'm always glad to hear from you, Sage," she said, totally out of character.

In all the years that he'd known Terra, she'd never sounded this upbeat over the phone. It was like she was a completely different person. Sage was as savvy as they came, and he couldn't help but think that her shift in attitude had to do with the movie studio. "Oh, I'm sure I have nothing to do with your good mood," he said, acting as if he were clueless. "So, what's going on? My secretary told me that you called."

"I was wondering if you're free tomorrow night. I've got two front row tickets to see Madonna, and tomorrow is the last night of her show. I remember how much you love her, so I thought you'd like to go."

Sage did love "The Material Girl." He'd seen her concert in London a few years ago and had a blast. "Thanks, I would love to go. What time should I pick you up?"

"I have an audition in midtown, so I'll pick you up from work around six o'clock, and we can grab a little dinner before going to the concert."

"Sounds good. See you then," Sage said and hung up.

She's definitely trying to schmooze me to get into one of my pictures, but I've got news for Ms. Benson. And it ain't good news, Sage thought as he swiveled around in his chair and glanced out of the picture window that overlooked midtown Manhattan.

8

TERRA CALLED ten ticket brokers, but they were all sold out. She should've known that it would be hard finding tickets to Madonna's concert at the last minute. She read about the concert in the newspaper and called Sage before she had the tickets in hand. The concert was the perfect excuse to see him again without seeming like she was scheming. Only now, Terra was beginning to panic. If she called him back and said that they were just going to dinner, he'd know that she had lied about the tickets. Terra's plan was to slowly change her attitude toward Sage. She had told him on more than one occasion that she thought of him as a "play brother," but now that he was heading up a major movie studio, "play brother" would soon be replaced with "lover." Terra wasn't worried about making the transition from friends to lovers. She knew that Sage absolutely adored her, and based on his feelings, she'd have him jumping through her designer hoops within weeks.

However, she still had to proceed with caution. Terra didn't want to blow her chances by acting too desperate.

"Hi, I'm calling to find out if you have tickets to see Madonna tonight?" she asked the eleventh ticket broker of the day.

"I only have four left," he said matter-of-factly.

Relieved, Terra exhaled loudly into the receiver. "I need two front row tickets."

"I don't got no front row seats. The closest I got to the stage is the fifth row. You want 'em or not?" he asked curtly.

Terra thought for a minute. She told Sage that she had front row seats; now if she showed up with fifth row seats, he would know that she didn't have the tickets when she'd called to invite him. On the other hand, fifth row was better than no row. "Yes, I'll take them," she said reluctantly. She was tempted to turn him down and call another broker, but based on her previous calls, this guy was probably her best bet. This was Madonna, after all, and the prime seats were obviously already gone.

"That'll be twenty-five hundred dollars. I take MasterCard, Visa, and AmEx. What card you gonna use?" he asked, getting right down to business.

"Twenty-five hundred dollars!" she shrieked. Terra could more than afford the tickets, but she'd rather pay twenty-five hundred dollars for a nice pair of boots instead of for a concert that would be over in a few hours. Though she was an heiress, she was frugal when it came to certain intangible things and extravagant with others like designer clothes, shoes, and handbags. She had a closet full of Birkin Bags, in a rainbow of colors, and with what she paid for the pricey Hermès purses, she could have easily funded a small third world village.

"Look, lady, I ain't got all day; either you want 'em or not, 'cause if you don't, someone else will easily take 'em off my hands," he said, trying to seal the deal.

"Yes, I want them." She took out her black AmEx and rattled off the numbers. "Can you have them messengered over to my apartment?"

"That'll cost you an extra fifty."

"Fifty dollars for a messenger?"

"You can come pick 'em up yourself or you can have them delivered, your choice."

Terra considered sending her driver, but she didn't want him getting caught up in midday traffic; it was already eleven forty-five and she had an audition at two-thirty, so sending him across town and back at this point was out of the question. She knew that the ticket broker was inflating the costs, but she had no choice. "Okay, add the delivery charge to my card," she said, and gave him her address.

The look for Terra's Dove audition was "All American," so she pulled her hair back in a tight knot, applied a thin layer of gloss to her lips, and dressed in a simple white shirtdress with mauve ballerina slippers. Her appearance was young and fresh, just like she had stepped off the pages of *Glamour*. Though her look was perfect for the audition, it was too straight-laced and boring for a Madonna concert. Terra threw a change of clothes in a tote bag, called her driver, and told him to meet her out front at one-thirty.

While she waited for the tickets to arrive, she read over the script that Feodora had faxed over earlier that morning. The lines were simple, and she repeated them in the mirror.

"Beauty this natural"—she rubbed the side of her cheek—"comes from only one beauty bar . . . Dove," she said, holding up a bar of soap and flashing a fresh smile.

As she repeated the line for the sixth time, the doorman rang up. "Ms. Benson, you have a package. Should I have him come up or shall I sign for you?"

"Sign for me, please, Jim. I'll be right down."

Terra grabbed the script and her tote bag and headed out the door. She picked up the envelope from her doorman, walked to the car, settled in the backseat, and pulled out the script, but before she could go over the lines again, her cell phone rang. "Hello?"

"Hey, Girl, what's up?" It was Lexi.

"I'm on my way to an audition, what are you up to?"

"I was calling to see if you wanted to grab lunch, and then go over to Barneys. My personal shopper called and said that the new Marc Jacobs bag is in, and I wanted to pick one up before they sell out." Lexington's life consisted of sleeping, shopping, partying, eating, and dating, not necessarily in that order. Her only ambition in life was to spend her parents' hard-earned money, and once she got married—in the very far future—she would then spend her husband's hard-earned money.

"I'd love to zip over to Barneys, but after the audition, I'm meeting Sage for dinner and then we're going to see Madonna at the Paramount."

"I tried to get tickets for that concert, but it was sold out. Sage must have ordered those tickets months ago." Lexi had every single one of Madonna's records and books. She loved everything about "The Material Girl," from her "I don't give a fuck" attitude to her choice of husbands. Lexi had the biggest crush on Guy Ritchie *and* Sean Penn.

"Sage didn't buy the tickets. I did," Terra told her.

"Why'd you do that? I thought he was so in love with you. Why isn't he wining and dining you like before? What happened?" Lexi asked, full of questions.

"Nothing happened. The tickets are just a lure to get him out. I told you I plan to charm my way right into his bed. I'm sick of going on these auditions, and Sage's new studio will be my salvation."

"When you're standing center stage at the Kodak Center accepting your Academy Award, don't forget to thank your girl for all the years of love and support," Lexi said, selfishly thinking about herself as always.

"Who's my girl?" Terra asked, teasing her.

"Don't be funny. I expect to be by your side at every red carpet event you attend. You know how I love the paparazzi!" she said with a smile in her voice.

"Lexi, I swear I've never seen anyone who loved being photographed more than you. I think you should hire a private coach and study acting, so you can attend the industry events on your own merit," Terra suggested.

"Girl, I'm not trying to work. I just want the glory without the guts. I'll leave pounding the pavement and going to auditions to you," she said cavalierly.

"Oh, I forgot that I was talking to Ms. Lazybones." Ever since they were kids, Lexington wasn't interested in anything but playing dress up and going to tea parties. Now that they were grown, the only thing that had changed was that the tea parties were at the Four Seasons, and she dressed in her own couture outfits instead of her mother's.

"I'm not lazy. I just prefer to spend my time having fun. Life's too short not to enjoy every single second," she said without shame.

"Life is short. That's why I'm taking the elevator straight to the top and skipping all of those unnecessary stops in between," Terra said.

"I heard that. Well, have fun tonight and let's get together before the week is over."

"Okay, talk to you later," Terra said, and flipped her phone shut.

The car was pulling up in front of the audition site on Forty-fourth and Broadway by the time Terra had finished her conversation with Lexington. She didn't have time to go over the lines again, so she stuffed the script back into her tote and climbed out of the car.

"Leroy, I don't know how long I'm going to be. This might take five minutes or five hours. You just never know with auditions," she told her driver.

"That's okay, Ms. Benson. I'll park over near Tenth Avenue, because the traffic around here is crazy," he said, looking out of the windshield at the gridlock in Times Square.

"I'll call you ten minutes before I'm ready to leave. That should give you plenty of time to get here," Terra said before walking into the building.

The auditions were being held at a casting agency on the sixteenth floor, and when Terra stepped off of the elevator, she gasped at the sight before her. Hundreds of beautiful girls were taking up every square inch of the hallway leading to the agency's door. There were blondes, brunettes, redheads, short hair, long hair, black, white, Asian, and Latina; every nationality under the sun seemed to be represented. They were all dressed similarly in white outfits with their hair pulled tightly into buns. Each face was scrubbed clean—with Dove soap no doubt—with only a thin layer of gloss on the lips. Terra thought that she had clinched the look of the "All American Girl," but every actress here had the same exact idea. She maneuvered her way to the receptionist.

"Hello, my name is Terra Benson and I have a two-thirty appointment with the casting director," she said haughtily.

"Here"—the receptionist handed her a number—"take this and wait your turn," she said, barely looking up.

Terra read the number "205" and put the orange ticket on the desk. "Excuse me, but I have an appointment. I'm not here for the cattle call."

"Look, this is an open casting, so either you wait or you leave. The choice is yours," the receptionist said in no uncertain terms.

FK hadn't said anything about an open casting. Terra was tempted to call her agent and tell her that she was leaving, but she knew that Feodora would be incensed. Besides, her days of waiting around for an audition would soon be over. She picked up the number and fought her way back near the elevators where there was room to breathe.

Nearly three hours later, her number was finally called, and she walked unenthusiastically into the audition room.

"Let me have your ticket," said the casting assistant. She then asked, "Do you have a head shot and résumé?"

Terra handed over the number, then reached into her bag and gave the woman her comp sheet. "Here you go."

The woman quickly looked it over and wrote "205" on the top left-hand corner. "Stand over there." She pointed to a black taped X on the floor. "State your name, and then speak your lines directly into the camera," she instructed.

Terra put her tote on the floor by the door, walked over to the X, straightened her shoulders, exhaled, said her name, and began her lines, "Beauty this natural"—she rubbed her cheek—"can only be Dove."

"Cut," yelled the director. "The line is 'Beauty this natural comes from only one beauty bar . . . Dove.' Not 'can only be Dove.' Run it again. Are you ready?" he asked Terra.

"Yes."

"Take two!" he yelled.

"Beauty this natural comes from Dove," she said, forgetting the rest of the line.

"Cut!" he yelled again. "You forgot to rub your face, and you forgot the rest of the line. Okay, this is your last chance," he spat out.

Terra was so nervous at this point that she jumbled up the lines and added a few new ones, "Dove is a natural beauty bar, and you can only get this face from Dove."

"Get her out of here! She's wasting my time," yelled the temperamental director. As Terra was leaving he added, "And next time learn your lines!"

Terra rushed over to the door, snatched up her tote bag, and nearly ran out of the room. She was beyond embarrassed. At home in front of the mirror she had the lines down cold, but in front of the camera, the words just wouldn't come out right. It was like she had some kind of unexpected stage fright. Terra jabbed at the elevator button. She wanted to escape with a quick exit but the elevator was taking forever. As she waited, she pulled out her cell phone and called Leroy.

"I'm ready. Get here as soon as you can."

"No problem, Ms. Benson. I'm on my way," he said and hung up.

When Terra reached the lobby, she pushed through the revolving doors and rushed out of the building, but Leroy was nowhere in sight. Traffic was gridlocked on Broadway and on Forty-fourth Street, and she realized that it would take him at least ten minutes to come across town.

"Damn, I should've called him twenty minutes ago," she said aloud, and began pacing the sidewalk like a madwoman.

The more she paced, the angrier she became. Walking blindly into an open call had rattled her nerves. She couldn't believe that she had blown a stupid commercial with only one line. Had Feodora told her it was a cattle call, she definitely would not have gone. She hated being grouped with the other wannabe starlets. Being an heiress, Terra was born with an innate sense of entitlement. Her last name held open doors that were closed to the masses, and she wasn't used to being treated like a commoner. *Well, once Sage gets his studio up and running, I won't have to subject myself to these humiliating cattle calls anymore.*

Terra stopped pacing and began to calm down. The more she thought about Sage's studio, the better she felt. She was so upset that she totally forgot to change her clothes. Terra dashed back into the building and noticed there was a ground-level café.

"May I use your restroom?" she asked the hostess.

"Sure. It's in the back, the first door to your right."

"Thank you," Terra said, and went straight to the back.

Fortunately it was one of those single private restrooms with a huge mirror and sink. Terra wasted no time making her transformation.

"Perfect," she commented to her reflection in the mirror. Satisfied with her look, she stuffed the boring audition clothes in her tote and headed for the door. Leroy was waiting curbside as she exited the building.

"Fifty-fourth and Park," she told him, and then pulled out her cell phone to call Sage. "Hey there," she said, once his secretary put her through. "I'm on my way. I should be there in about ten."

"Okay. I'll be downstairs."

"I was thinking that we could grab a quick bite at Bryant Park Grill, and then head over to the Garden," she suggested.

"Sounds good. See you in ten," he said, and hung up.

Terra used the final minutes before picking him up to tweak her makeup and hair. She spritzed her neck with L'Heure Magique, and then sprayed the delicious scent between her boobs, just in case things got steamy and Sage wanted a little more than a good night kiss after the concert.

The car was pulling up just as Sage was exiting his Park Avenue office. He spotted Terra's silver Maybach sitting curbside and walked over to the car. The driver greeted him on the passenger side and opened the door.

"Hey, you." Terra smiled happily.

Sage opened his mouth to speak, but was stunned into silence by Terra's appearance. Her usual sophisticated, couture-suit, pearl-clad look was replaced by ripped jeans, a black leather bustier, and five-inch stilettos. Her hair, which was normally pulled back in a chignon, was loose and wavy, giving her a wild, East Village type vibe. Usually she only wore a pat of lip gloss and a light dusting of translucent powder, but tonight her lips were ruby red, her eye-lashes were layered with mascara, and her cheeks were rosy from blush. Sage didn't know what to say; it was as if he were looking at a totally different person. He had never seen her look so vibrant and alive. Not that he didn't like the old Terra, but this new and improved version was much better. Now that she had literally let her hair down, maybe they could finally have some fun. "Wow," he said, "I like the new look."

"Thanks." She leaned over and kissed him on the cheek. "Since we're going to see Madonna, I wanted to blend in and not stand out in one of my Chanel suits." She chuckled. In truth, Terra could care less about blending in. The only reason why she was dolled up was to catch Sage's eye. And apparently it was working. He was looking at her from her carefree hairdo to her pointed-toe shoes. *It's just a matter of time before I have him drinking my golden pee,* she thought, and smiled ever so slightly. Terra gave Leroy the ad-dress of the restaurant, and within ten minutes they were pulling up in front of Bryant Park Grill.

A jazz rendition of James Blunt's "Beautiful" was playing softly in the background as they made their way to the hostess podium. Terra gave her name and they were seated immediately. The waiter promptly came over, took their water request, and described the spe-cials for the evening.

"Tonight we have roasted lobster chowder, and for our entrée, the chef has prepared braised short ribs marinated in cognac served with a medley of baby vegetables and whipped potatoes."

"That sounds good, but I'd like to look over the menu," Terra told the waiter.

"Can I bring you cocktails while you're deciding?"

"Yes, I'll have a Belvedere martini with a twist," she said.

Sage looked at her strangely. He had never known Terra to drink anything stronger than champagne. He ordered the same, and once the waiter was gone, he asked, "Since when did you start drinking vodka?"

"I've been drinking vodka since college," she said casually, as if it were no big deal.

"I didn't know that."

She shrugged her shoulders and said suggestively, "There's a lot about me you don't know."

Sage smiled at the thought of seeing a different side of Terra. She had always presented to him her conservative side, but tonight the debutante was gone, replaced by a young vibrant spirit. He was thrilled at the prospect of getting to know Terra the rebel. Sage had dreamed of the day when she would see him in a different light, and not as a pseudo brother, and from the way she was beaming at him from across the table, it seemed that that day had finally come. *Maybe she is into me, and not just after a movie role,* he thought.

"Sooo," she said, nearly purring, "what's going on with the studio?" She reached across the table and stroked the top of his hand.

I should've known this was coming, he thought. Sage eased his hand away from hers. "It's a work in progress," he responded in a deadpan tone. Sage despised being manipulated, and suddenly didn't feel like going to the concert. He excused himself to the men's room, called his secretary at home, and told her to call him on his cell in five minutes. When he returned to the table, Terra was sitting erect, with her back arched and her boobs pointed forward, nearly spilling out of the bustier, trying to entice him.

"I ordered the pumpkin ravioli as an appetizer. It's delicious. I'm sure you'll love it." She smiled warmly.

"Sounds good. I love pum . . ." Before he could finish the sentence, his phone buzzed inside of his breast pocket. "Excuse me," he said, and answered the call. "Hello? . . . What? . . . Why didn't you call me earlier? . . . Okay, okay, I'll be right there," he said urgently, and flipped the phone shut.

Terra saw the look of panic on his face. "Is everything okay?"

"It's my dad. He's been rushed to the hospital," he lied. "I hate to run out on you, but I need to go and find out what happened. I'm so sorry about dinner and the concert." He stood up to leave.

"Don't worry about it. Why don't I go with you?" she offered.

"No, no, that's not necessary. I'm sure it's nothing serious. Stay and enjoy dinner." He kissed her on the cheek. "Have a good time at the concert. I'll call you later." And with that, he was headed for the door.

Terra sat there dumbfounded, and watched his retreating back as he fled the restaurant, leaving her standing there speechless.

9

MISSY AND two of her stripper friends from Scores were at
BD2 to let their hair down after a hard night's work. At the Black
Door, they didn't have to slither their bodies down a chrome pole,
or give endless lap dances to horny men begging for a little attention, or fend off unwanted advances from love-starved husbands.
Here they were the clients and their only job was to have a good
time. They didn't have to worry about convincing a client to spend
hundreds of dollars in the VIP room to make their quota. If they
chose to fuck a server or two, the decision was totally up to them.
Since Missy and her friends worked in the adult entertainment
business, they were offered a special discounted membership, as an
industry courtesy. Missy was so busy with work and her extracurricular activities that she'd only been to the club a couple of times,
and had yet to experience all of the chambers that BD2 had to offer. On her previous visits, she'd danced the night away in the Studio 54-like disco, but tonight she and her friends were starving, so

before letting their hair down on the dance floor, they decided to go to the Aphrodisiac Bistro and grab some much needed fuel.

The food in the Aphrodisiac Bistro wasn't the only enticing element; the decor was just as stimulating. Crush burgundy velvet, high-backed booths lined the perimeter, and in the center of the intimate room was a buffet featuring oysters on the half shell, escargot, mussels in black truffle oil, fresh asparagus, and chocolate-dipped bananas. A statue of a Greek god stood at the end of the six-foot-long buffet with an erect penis, from which champagne flowed freely. There were no bright lights, only vanilla-scented candles to heighten the senses, giving the entire room a plush and sexy vibe.

"Hmm, these oysters are to die for," Luscious said, slipping a mollusk off the shell into her mouth.

Princess was busy sucking down her own oyster and nodded her head in agreement. Missy, Luscious, and Princess—not their real names of course—started dancing at Scores around the same time, and since they were all newbies, they joined forces and became fast friends. Until she started dancing at Scores, Missy's life had been full of high drama and turmoil. She wanted different things in life and her family just didn't understand her blind ambition, so instead of accepting her, they shut her out. Immediately after college graduation, she left her small Illinois town and headed east to New York in the hopes of furthering her dance career. She auditioned for chorus roles in Broadway musicals. She even auditioned for a Rockette spot at Radio City, but didn't make the cut. With her savings quickly dwindling, Missy heard about an opening at Scores. Working at a strip joint was not her first choice, but she had no other options. The moment Missy entered the club for the audition she realized that Scores was not some sleazy strip joint, but a classy gentlemen's club. With a BA in dance, Missy's moves were off the chain, and within a few months she had regulars who came to the club just to see her perform. And for the first time in her life, she felt at home.

"You can have those slimy oysters." She turned her nose up in disgust. "I prefer seven inches of chocolate perfection," Missy said, sucking the tip of a chocolate-covered banana as if she were giving head.

"All you think about is dick," said Luscious. "Either you're talking about how some dude fucked you up the ass, or how you sucked the cum right out of his pee hole."

"Don't get mad at me 'cause you're a dyke and don't like dick," Missy shot back.

"I ain't mad. I just get tired of you talking about men. Is that all you think about?" Luscious pinned her with a questioning look.

"If it wasn't for my skills at giving good head, I would have never made it through college," Missy told her.

"What do you mean by that?" Princess asked.

"It's a long story. I'll tell you some other time, but tonight I want to find a server with a dick as pretty and perfect as this banana so I can suck him off. The only aphrodisiac I have a taste for tonight is some hot creamy cum," Missy stated, and scanned the room for a victim.

Luscious rolled her eyes. "I'll see you all later. I'm going to the Pink Room for a little fun." The Pink Room was where the lesbians usually congregated.

"I don't know why you have to get her riled up. You know she hates talking about men," Princess said once Luscious had walked away.

"If she hates men so much, why in the hell is she working at Scores, where men paw at her all night long?"

"Because the money is good, that's why. Isn't that why we're all there?" Princess asked, turning the question back to Missy.

Missy hesitated a second. "I guess you have a point. But trust me, my days of stripping for a living are almost over. Once I save enough money, I'm outta there," she stated with conviction.

Princess had heard that line at least a million times, and was unimpressed. Every stripper she knew had a plan to quit the business—a plan that never materialized—including herself. "Isn't that what we all say?"

Missy could hear the skepticism in her friend's voice, but instead of detailing her exit strategy, she chose to take the fifth. "Now that one looks like he's packing," she said, changing the subject and nodding in the direction of a masked, buffed server wearing a snug wife-beater and an even snugger pair of blue jeans.

Mason saw the two gorgeous women standing at the buffet and slowly strutted toward them. He dreamed about the woman he met at Borders, and had woken up that morning with a massive hard-on. He tried all day to suppress his lustful feelings, but his dick had other plans. Now he was on the prowl again, looking for a little action. The women both wore elaborate masks. The taller of the two had on a multicolored mask with long pink, yellow, teal, red, and tangerine plumes adorning each side. The shorter woman's mask was pewter with gold and black feathers near the top and bottom of her eyes, and from a distance the feathers looked like giant eyelashes.

"Ladies, are you having a good time?" Mason asked once he had made his way over to where they stood.

Missy looked at his well-defined pecs and the imprint of his ripped six-pack, and said, "It could be better."

"How so?" Mason prided himself on accommodating his clientele, and was anxious to hear comments on ways to improve the club.

"Well for starters—" Missy slowly walked around him, sizing up his goods. She could see a hefty bulge protruding through his jeans. From experience, she knew some men had heavy balls that made it appear as if they had long dongs, but that wasn't always the case. "—how big is your dick?"

Mason chuckled slightly. He hadn't expected her to say that, but this was the Black Door and just about anything was said *and* done within the confines of these walls. "It's big enough to choke a horse," he said confidently.

"Well, I'm not a horse, but I assure you I won't choke while I'm going down on your dick," Missy said, rubbing her hand against his crotch.

Mason felt his manhood spring to life at her touch. "Is that a fact?"

"It's more than a fact; it's a promise."

"Promises are made to be kept, and not broken," he teased back.

She grabbed his hand. "Let's go back to one of the booths. I can show you better than I can tell you."

As they started to walk away, Princess spoke up. "Don't leave me out; I wanna cum too!"

Mason took her hand. "Don't worry, Honey; I got enough dick for the both of you."

The three of them walked hand in hand to an empty booth, but instead of settling in at the table, the women sat Mason down and stood over him. Missy unbuckled his belt, unzipped his jeans, and took out his swollen cock. She then got on her knees and took his bulbous head into her mouth. Princess slid her tube top down to her waist, allowing her surgically enhanced titties to spring loose. She leaned over so that her nipples brushed his lips. Mason reached up and grabbed both of her titties and began sucking one and then the other. Her nipples were burgeoning into hardness with each lick of his tongue. Mason was a breast man, and he loved to feel a woman's nipples harden inside of his wet mouth.

With one woman on her knees and one feeding him her ripe breasts, Mason was in carnal heaven. He closed his eyes and behind his lids lurid bursts of red, orange, and purple exploded like fireworks on the Fourth of July. This was a man who truly loved his job and the perks that came with it! Though he had vowed to stop fucking around with the clients, his libido seemed to be in perpetual overdrive and until he had a steady girlfriend, that was one promise that would be broken again and again. Mason lifted his hips off of the seat so that he could feed her every inch of his rod. "Suck that big dick and make it cum," he demanded.

Missy had to admit that he had one of the biggest cocks that she had ever seen. There was something familiar about his cock, but she couldn't put her finger on it. She had sucked so many dicks in her lifetime that identifying one without seeing the face attached to it was futile, so she put the thought out of her mind and continued to enjoy herself.

"Oh, yeah, I'm—cumming," Mason moaned.

"Squirt . . . your creamy cum . . . right down my throat," Missy said in between sucks.

Mason loved a woman who wasn't afraid to swallow. Most women held the semen in their mouth and pretended to swallow but this chick seemed to be the real deal. As he released his white hot load, he opened his eyes and waited for her to spit out his life-giving juices, but she greedily swallowed every single drop. "Was the dick big enough for you?" he asked once she stood up.

"Big and tasty." Missy smiled, and wiped the back of her mouth with her hand.

"And how were the tits?" Princess asked.

"Big and tasty," Mason said, repeating Missy's words.

"Well, I hope you ladies are having a better time now." He smiled and zipped up his jeans.

"Much better!" they said in unison.

"We aim to please at BD Two, so spread the word to all your girlfriends," Mason said, using his best sales pitch voice.

"I'll remember that the next time I wanna suck some good dick," Missy said, looking down at Mason's crotch, then she and Princess strolled out of the bistro in search of another well-hung server to double-team.

10

THE MORNING breeze off of the Hudson filled Mason's lungs as he made his usual trek from Seventy-second Street up to Ninety-sixth Street and back. After a night of carousing at the club, he needed to clear his head, and a jog along the river was just what the doctor ordered. Mason had gotten off track, and was seeking out sex at the club when he should have been upstairs in his office doing paperwork. His brain seemed to be residing in the head between his legs, instead of in the head on his neck. When he left the club in the wee hours of the morning after having an oral ménage à trois with two women—and his brain was back where it belonged—he swore to himself that that would be the last time he used BD2 for his personal pleasure. He'd seen firsthand how Trey's life was almost destroyed after having a torrid affair with a client and he didn't want to suffer the same fate. Mason needed an anchor to keep him from drifting back into the decadent waters of the club, but there were no buoys in sight.

After his run, he was drenched with salty sweat and headed home to shower and change. Mason dressed in his signature Seven jeans, put on a starched white, French-cuffed shirt, but let the cuffs hang loose past his wrists, for an urban casual look. He slipped on a pair of black Gucci loafers sans socks. He slapped his freshly shaven cheeks with aftershave, grabbed his wallet, planted it inside his back pocket, and headed out the door. Mason was craving his daily dose of double espresso so he walked two short blocks to Borders. On his way to the bookstore, he passed up a Starbucks on the corner of Seventy-fourth and Broadway. He could have easily bought his jolt of java there, but what he wanted wasn't at Starbucks or at the corner coffee shop. What he craved could only be had at Borders.

The bookstore café was crowded as usual, and Mason scanned the patrons as he stood in line, but she wasn't there. Ever since he met "The Mystery" woman a week ago—well, he hadn't officially met her—he'd been coming back to Borders in the hopes of getting a proper introduction, but she hadn't been around. Mason regretted not engaging her in a conversation when he had had the chance, but that day in his jogging gear he was sweaty and scruffy, and shied away from introducing himself. The way he looked she probably thought that he was a lowlife scrub. Ever since then, he rushed home after his run, showered, and changed. In the event he saw her again, he wanted her to see how well he cleaned up.

"A double espresso, and a poppy-seed muffin," he told the cashier when he stepped up to the counter. After the cashier gave him his morning pick-me-up, he walked toward the tables to find a seat.

There she is, Mason said to himself as he spotted the back of a woman wearing a canary yellow blouse with a matching sweater tied around her shoulders. He almost tripped over his own feet as he rushed over to the table.

"Excuse me, is this seat taken?" he asked, smiling and exposing his perfect chalk white teeth.

The woman turned around, looked up at Mason, and said, "No, it's not." She moved her tote out of the seat so that he could sit down.

His heart dropped when he looked into her face. It wasn't his "Mystery Woman" but a replica. From the back, the women were identical, but up close and personal, there was a marked difference. This chick had a face only a mother could love. Her teeth—what was left of them—were crooked. Her skin was a canvas of red pimples and unsightly pockmarks. Her only redeeming feature was her hair; it was long and wavy. But upon closer inspection, Mason realized that it was a bad weave.

"Hi, I'm Beatrice," she said, extending her hand to him.

Mason reluctantly shook her hand. "Hi, Beatrice." He purposely didn't offer his name in return. He just stood there looking dumbfounded. He'd made a colossal mistake and didn't know how to extract himself from the situation without seeming rude.

"Here"—she motioned to the chair—"sit down."

The last thing Mason wanted to do was to sit. He wanted to sprint out the door. But since he had asked if the seat was empty in the first place, he sat down so he wouldn't seem schizophrenic.

"Do you live in the neighborhood?" she asked the second he sat down.

"Uh," he hesitated, "yeah."

"Can you tell me where the nearest cleaners is? I just moved here from Mississippi, and I can't find a good cleaners, shoe repair guy, or a decent market. This city is so big and confusing that I'm having a hard time finding my way around. I'm used to country roads and friendly faces." She smiled, exposing her beat-up grill.

Mason wanted to say, *Maybe you need to go back to the country.*

But instead he said, "Coliseum Cleaners is half a block away, going south. It's on the east side of the street. You can't miss the bright red awning."

She looked confused. "On the south side of the street, going east?"

"No, on the east side of street, going south," he repeated.

"Do you mind showing me after you finish your coffee?" she asked in a helpless damsel-in-distress southern accent.

Mason nearly choked on his espresso. He wouldn't be seen dead with the likes of her. "I'm sorry, but I have to run," he said, abruptly getting up from the table. Before she could utter another word, he was taking giant steps toward the door with his coffee in hand. He knew he was being rude, but at this point he really didn't care, all he cared about was putting some distance between him and Ms. Southern Belle.

"Watch it!" Terra shouted as Mason ran into her with his open cup of espresso, spilling the hot coffee down the front of her shirt.

He had been so busy trying to escape that he hadn't paid much attention to where he was going. "Excuse me," he said, looking into the face of his intended prey.

Terra reached into her tote bag, quickly retrieved a handkerchief, and dabbed at the coffee stain, trying in vain to absorb the dark liquid before it ruined her bright white shirt.

Mason looked at the coffee collage on her blouse and began to apologize profusely. "I'm so sorry. I didn't see you. I'm so sorry," he repeated. "Let me get you some seltzer water so it won't stain," he said, and rushed over to the counter.

When he came back with a bottle of Perrier, Terra was sitting at a window table, rubbing the stain with her monogrammed handkerchief. "They didn't have any seltzer, but I thought that this would work just as well," he said, drenching a napkin with the carbonated water and handing it to her. He wanted to rub the spot himself, but it was right near her breasts, and he didn't want to get slapped in the face for being out of line.

She took the napkin. "Thanks."

Mason watched her dab away at the stain; the more she soaked her blouse, the more transparent it got. It was like having his own private wet T-shirt contest. His eyes were glued to her every movement, and when he saw her nipples peak through the sheer bra that she wore, his lethargic dick woke up. Mason wanted to rip her blouse off and suck her nipples right there in Borders. She was just the type of anchor—beautiful and sexy—that he needed to keep him from straying into the bowels of BD2. He picked up another napkin and poured the rest of the Perrier on it. "Here, let me. It's the least I can do," he offered anyway, hoping she wouldn't refuse.

Terra pushed his hand away. "No thanks, I've got this," she said in a terse voice as she shot him the evil eye.

She didn't seem like the type who was into small talk, so Mason didn't bother. "At least let me buy you another shirt," he said as a peace offering.

Terra loved white shirts, and had a closet full of them in different styles and fabrics. "No thanks, that won't be necessary," she replied, taking in his appearance for the first time. He too had on a white shirt. The last time she'd seen him, he was less than appealing in a tattered T-shirt and baggy sweatpants, but today he was cleanly shaven, smelling good, and casually dressed. He was just her type—tall, handsome, and well groomed.

"Well, if I can't buy you a blouse, the least I can do is buy you dinner," he said, smiling like a schoolboy.

Terra was tempted to take him up on his offer, but she declined. Though he was fine as hell, she wasn't interested in getting to know a random stranger. She needed to use all of her energy to rope in Sage. "No thank you." She stood up. "Excuse me, but I need to go home and change," she said, holding the handkerchief against the stain.

She walked briskly out of the café before Mason could get her information, but he had her number all right—she was the stuck-up, hard-to-get type—and he'd have to work a little harder to get her attention. Wooing a sophisticated woman like that would be challenging, but the victory would be well worth the fight.

11

SAGE WAS up to his perfectly groomed neck in architects, floor plans, and contractors. The reconstruction of the soundstage located in Long Island City, just east of Manhattan, was consuming nearly eighty percent of his day, and it was nearly impossible to fit his other responsibilities as CEO in the remaining twenty percent. He was tempted to hire a consultant to oversee the project, but this was *his* baby, and he wanted to be hands-on in every single phase of development.

"Yeah, Roy, I have the drawings right here on my desk." Sage was on the phone with the chief architect for the renovation. Roy Snyderman was the best in the business, and being the best he was in high demand and traveled throughout the country consulting with clients and overseeing projects. He had offices in New York, Beverly Hills, and London.

"So tell me, what do you think?" Roy asked, pleased with the work he had done.

"What do I think?" Sage repeated the question. "I think this is not what we discussed. I told you to design four state-of-the-art sets, and I only see two in the drawings." Sage drummed the white tip of his black Mont Blanc on the architectural drawings and huffed into the phone.

"That's because the soundstage isn't large enough to accommodate four separate sets. Unless you want four tiny, closetlike sets, there's only space for two. So I used my discretion and designed two spacious, functional sets," Roy stated, firmly holding his ground.

"When are you coming back East?" Roy was in his West Coast office working with executives from Universal on a new project. "We need to sit down and go over my vision again, because clearly it's skewed," Sage spat into the receiver, sounding completely disgusted.

"I'm leaving for London tomorrow and won't be back until late next week. In the interim, you can meet with Susan Bergman, my VP of Design, and go over any revisions you have," Roy said calmly. He dealt with temperamental clients on a daily basis, and was unfrazzled by Sage's curtness. He then added, "But unless you want to build on extra square footage, the existing building will only yield two sets."

Sage didn't have any intention on meeting with Roy's underling, so he ignored the comment and asked, "How long would it take to add on an extension?"

"We're talking at least six to eight additional months. We'll need to draw up new plans and have them approved by—"

Sage cut him off, "That's entirely too long. I plan to have the studio up and running before the end of the year."

"Well in that case, I suggest you stick with the original plans, since they've already been approved, and construction is under way," he said, giving Sage a dose of reality.

Sage sighed heavily. His vision was being compromised, and he didn't like it, not one little bit. He was Sage Hirschfield and Sage Hirschfield rarely made concessions. "Let me think about this," he said as he sighed again.

"Don't think too long, because if we're going to scrap these plans and start over from square one, we'll need to move ASAP," Roy said, sounding as cool as an autumn breeze.

"Understood. I'll be in touch," Sage answered curtly, and pressed the speakerphone button, disconnecting the call, without saying good-bye.

Out of frustration, Sage suddenly grabbed the drawings off his desk and began balling them up with his fists. He swiveled around in his chair and threw the crumpled pieces of paper one by one against the floor-to-ceiling windows that overlooked Park Avenue. He hadn't anticipated this little snafu, and was pissed. He wanted desperately to prove to his father that he could stand on his own two feet without being propped up by the family legacy. "Fuck!" he yelled at the top of his lungs. Sage began to count to twenty to cool his jets. He needed to blow off some steam, and he knew just who to call to relieve the stress. He turned back to his desk, picked up the receiver—because this was one conversation he didn't want broadcast through the speakerphone—and dialed Missy.

"Hey, Baby," she cooed into the phone. With caller ID, she didn't have to pretend like she didn't know who was on the other end.

Her sexy voice began to instantly calm him down. "How's that fine ass of yours doing?" he asked, getting straight to the point.

"Tight and waiting for you," she purred.

"What are you wearing?"

"A thin white T-shirt, without a bra, so my titties are loose and free, and a tight, pink thong."

"Go into the bathroom, turn on the cold water, cup your hands underneath the faucet, and put that ice-cold water on your T-shirt until it's soaked," he instructed.

"Okay, Baby, whatever you say." After a few seconds, Missy said, "Ohh, it's sooo cold."

"Look in the mirror. Can you see your nipples through the shirt?"

"Yeah, Baby, I can see 'em."

"Are they hard yet?" Sage asked, envisioning the silhouette of her round nipples.

"Oh, yeah, they're so hard they're poking through the shirt. Oh, Baby, you should see how tasty they look."

Sage closed his eyes and imagined Missy standing in front of the mirror wearing a wet T-shirt, with her double Ds showing through. He loved playing with her voluptuous rack. It was probably saline-enhanced, but he didn't care; these days it was no big deal since most women had implants. "Play with your nipples for me, and then reach down and suck them through the wet shirt."

Missy made a smacking sound as if she were sucking her own nipples. "Ohhh, they taste sooo good," she purred.

At the thought of her sucking on those big ass titties, Sage's dick twitched inside of his silk boxers.

"Are you hard yet, Baby?" Missy asked instinctively.

"I'm getting there," he said, putting his hand on his heated crotch.

"Mr. Hirschfield," his secretary called his name through the intercom before he had a chance to release his throbbing cock, "Ms. Benson is on two."

"Hold on, Missy," he said, and pressed the intercom button. "I can't talk to her now, and hold all of my calls for the next thirty minutes," he said abruptly and disconnected the intercom.

"Now where were we?" he asked, returning his attention back to Missy.

"I was just going to tell you to take out that big dick. Can you do that for me?" she asked, turning the tables and taking control.

"Yeah, Baby." Sage unzipped his pants and eased out his turgid erection.

"Are you holding *my* dick?"

"Yeah, Baby, I'm holding *your* dick."

"I want you to close your eyes and stroke it up and down. Keep stroking it up and down, and up and down until it stands at attention. How does that feel?"

"Ohh, it feels goooddd!"

"Now grip it as tight as you can, and imagine you sticking that hard pole in my tight little ass. Imagine the head pushing through first; ease that rod in slowly. Now my asshole is gripping your dick so tight causing you to ooze a little pre-cum. But don't cum just yet. I need for you to punish my ass 'cause I've been a bad girl. Now . . . RAM IT, MOTHERFUCKER!" she yelled into the phone.

Sage increased the pressure on his cock and began stroking faster and faster, as if he were inside of her. "Take that, you dirty bitch," he grunted.

"Is that all you got, you filthy bastard?"

"Bend over and spread those cheeks, Bitch, because I'm going to rip your hole wide open," he said in a hushed tone so his secretary couldn't hear.

"Bring it on, you dirty motherfucker, because I'm primed and ready for a good ass fuck," she hissed into the phone.

His sensory memory took over, and he could feel her tight ass as if he were deep inside. He tightened his grip and pulled his dick from the base to the tip and back again. Missy was the only woman he knew who preferred to be butt-fucked instead of the old-fashioned way, and he loved every minute of it. Sage could cum in her ass without worrying about making any babies. He kept stroking and stroking until he felt that undeniable urge to cum. "Oh, shit, I'm cumming. I'm cumming." He let out a shriek as a river of semen rushed out of his tiny hole, onto his hand, and was absorbed into his gabardine slacks.

Knowing she had completed a job well done, Missy purred, "Was it good, Baby?"

Sage was still breathless. "You're . . . the . . . best," he said in between gasps of air.

"And don't you ever forget it!"

"I gotta run, Missy. I'll talk to you later," he said, ending their afternoon sex session, and put the phone back in its cradle.

Now that he had bust a serious nut, he could concentrate on solving the dilemma at hand, but before any business could be conducted Sage needed to change his pants because the cum had made an unsightly chalky mark. As he walked into his private bathroom with adjoining closet, he thought about Terra. Seeing her dressed like a party girl the other night in low-cut jeans and a provocative leather bustier, he couldn't help but wonder if she was as wild as Missy. He wondered if he could call her a dirty bitch while fucking her up the ass, or if she would suck his dick until he squirted cum down her throat. The more he thought about it, the more he realized that Terra was just playing dress up for the night, and the combination of name calling and lewd sex was not her flavor; she was too well bred for such raunchy seduction.

12

"SO WHAT happened the other night? You never called me
with an update," Lexington said to Terra. They were having a girls'
night out. After a wonderful dinner at Sapa, a French/Vietnamese
hot spot in Chelsea, they were having after-dinner drinks at Pravda,
a vodka bar in NoLiTa.

"I was wondering when you were going to ask." Terra chuckled. "You went through an entire meal without interrogating me."

"Excuse me, but I didn't think asking about a friend's life was
considered an interrogation," Lexington said, slightly irritated.

"Pull the claws back in, I was just kidding. I didn't call you because there's really nothing to tell," Terra said matter-of-factly.

"What do you mean? I thought you had a big night planned
with Sage. How was the concert? Was 'The Material Girl' dancing
her ass off as usual?" Lexington wanted to know.

"I couldn't tell you," Terra said casually, taking a sip of her
chilled Russian vodka.

Lexington looked at her strangely. "What do you mean?"

"We didn't go to the concert."

"Why?" Lexington pinned her with a questioning stare. "I thought you said you got the tickets."

"I did get the tickets; spent twenty-five hundred dollars on them as a matter of fact," Terra said, still upset at wasting money on the unused tickets. "But Sage had to leave as soon as we got to the restaurant because his father had been rushed to the emergency room. So to answer your question, nothing happened because he left before the night got started."

"How is his father? Hope it wasn't anything serious." Lexington knew the elder Hirschfield from her childhood and admired his accomplishments.

"I don't know. I called his office yesterday, but his secretary said he was on a conference call, and he hasn't called me back yet. It's not like Sage not to return my call right away. I hope everything's okay," Terra said, beginning to worry.

"Call him now and find out what's going on," Lexington suggested.

"Good idea." Terra took out her phone and called Sage's cell, but after five rings, it went into voice mail. "Hey, it's me. I was calling to find out how your dad is doing. Call me back," Terra said, leaving him a message.

"Well, let's hope everything's okay," Lexington said, picking up her vodka rocks and draining the last drop from the glass.

"Yeah, let's hope."

"Can I get you ladies another round?" asked the handsome, hunky bartender.

"Absolutely!" Lexington winked, flirting with the Terrence Howard look-alike. She glanced around the cozy room with its low ceiling, overstuffed leather chairs, and intimate booths. Pravda drew some of the prettiest people in the city, and was popular with the late-night crowd. "There are some fine men here tonight," she said, spotting a group of Abercrombie & Fitch–looking models.

Terra swiveled slightly on the bar stool and took a peek. "They're cute, but they look like teenagers. I like my men a bit more seasoned."

"Like Professor Langston?" Lexington asked, pinning Terra with a knowing look.

In her junior year of college, Terra had an affair with her drama professor. David Langston was just out of graduate school and only a few years older than Terra. He was an aspiring actor himself and had the movie-star good looks to go along with his skills. He was six feet three inches, slim, with Belgian chocolate skin and honey-colored eyes. David was distracted by Terra's beauty the moment she stepped into his class and he tried his best to ignore the attraction he felt for her. He kept his libido in check until the day he had to help her with a love scene. Terra was having a hard time kissing her acting partner passionately. They were portraying star-crossed lovers, but her kiss was lukewarm at best. David stopped the action, stepped on the stage, swept Terra into his arms, and kissed her, tongue and all. He held her tight in his arms until he felt her respond. His mission was to show the class how to deliver a passionate kiss, but he wasn't acting. His kiss was real.

Terra had never been kissed like that before, and his kiss unleashed a desire in her that she never knew existed, and she wanted more. Terra got his address from the department secretary—under the guise of dropping off an overdue paper—and showed up on his doorstep unannounced, but not unwelcomed.

David opened his door and didn't say one word. He just pulled her inside and shut the door. He untied the belt on her trench coat as if he were unwrapping an unexpected gift. He unbuttoned her jeans and slid them past her slim hips. He then got on his knees and kissed her from her ankles to her inner thighs, up to her silk panties. He kissed the front of the panties until they were saturated from his moist mouth. Terra tried to squirm away, but he reached up and grabbed her ass, pulling her in closer. He tore off the panties with his teeth, found her clit, and began sucking it feverishly.

Terra thought she was going to lose her mind. Having been sheltered all of her life, she was still a virgin and had never even had oral sex before, and the sensation felt so good, so good in fact that she began peeing on herself. David sucked the golden liquid out of her pee hole and drank it up as if it were a delicious nectar.

Once she had released a series of orgasms, he got off of his knees, pulled down his sweatpants, took his erect cock, and rubbed it against her clit. He then turned her around and bent her over slightly so that he could enter her from behind. Her pussy was so tight that he reached around with one hand and stuck two fingers inside to loosen her up. He then guided his hard cock into her sacred walls and began to gently rock back and forth. He sensed that she was a virgin because she didn't return his rhythm. He whispered for her to push back against his dick; he then held her by the waist until she found her rhythm. He began to slowly fuck her with long even strokes. David wanted to take his time and show her how to move her body like a pro. He plunged deep on the in stroke, and then pulled out until the rim of his head kissed the opening of her V-spot. She shuttered from the sensation, but quickly caught on and bucked back until they were fucking in sync.

David tutored Terra all night and half the morning on the art of sucking, fucking, licking, and swallowing. He showed her positions only a contortionist could perform, but she managed to twist her body to accommodate his commands. Her sexual appetite was insatiable and he fed her until her pussy ached. David transformed Terra from an inexperienced girl who knew nothing into a woman who knew how to please herself as well as her partner. They continued their affair until David left teaching and moved to L.A. to star in a B-movie.

"David Langston." Terra smiled and licked her lips. "Now that's a man who knows how to please a woman. I haven't had sex like that since he moved to Hollywood over a year ago."

"That's a shame." Lexington shook her head. "Girl, my world isn't right unless I cum on a weekly basis. And speaking of cumming, I'll bet he can suck the hell out of a clit. Look at his mouth." She motioned to a tall, bald brother with full kissable lips.

Terra turned slightly and looked across the room. She turned back quickly. "I know him," she whispered.

"How do you know *him*? He's too fine," Lexington asked, looking directly at Mason, trying to make eye contact.

"Well, I don't know him know him. I met him at Borders."

"Really." Lexington smiled. "What's his name?" she asked, ready for an introduction.

"Well, I didn't really meet him, I—"

Lexington cut her off. "Wait a minute, what's the deal? You don't know him know him, and you don't know his name either? Well, in that case, I'd say he's open prey; every woman for herself," Lexington said, and smiled in Mason's direction.

"Go for it," Terra said unresponsively. She was used to Lexington trying to snap up every good-looking man she laid her eyes on, and wasn't in the mood to compete.

"Excuse me, ladies, but the gentleman over there has bought you a bottle of Belvedere," the bartender said, nodding toward Mason.

Lexington turned back toward Mason and waved him over. While he was making his way through the crowded room, Lexington quickly took out her lip gloss and smeared the shiny goo on her lips. She straightened her posture so that her tits sprang forward in her tight-fitting low-cut top. "Thanks for the vodka." She batted

her eyes as he stood directly in front of Terra's stool. "I'm Lexi"—
she extended her hand—"and this is my friend, Terra."

Mason barely looked at Lexington because his eyes were glued
to Terra. "Finally, a proper introduction," he said to her.

"Not really," Terra responded glibly, "because I still don't know
your name."

"My bad." He grinned. "I'm Mason Anthony." He reached for
her hand, and held it in his for a brief second before letting it go.

"So, Mason," Lexington said, interrupting their vibe, "what do
you do?"

"I'm into real estate," he said, with a ready answer. Trey had
schooled him on what to say when that question came up. It was a
partial truth, since they were always scouting properties to convert
into another Black Door. Though one of his duties at the club was
to recruit new members, he had to use his discretion, and Terra
didn't look like she belonged at the Black Door.

"Oh, are you an agent?" Lexington asked.

"No," he said, preferring not to elaborate. "And what about
you?" He returned his attention to Terra. "What do you do?"

"I'm an actress," she said proudly, as if she were already a star.

"Oh, yeah?" His eyes lit up. She was so beautiful that he should
have known that she was in the entertainment industry. "Would I
have seen you in anything?"

"Not unless you go to auditions," Lexington butted in. "She's
still trying to land the role of a lifetime." She laughed as if she had
just told the funniest joke.

Terra cut Lexi a "don't even go there" look, and said, "It's true,
I'm still pounding the pavement, but it's just a matter of time before you see my face on the silver screen."

I'd love to see your face in my bed, he thought. "Move over,
Halle." He smiled. "Here comes Terra."

Terra blushed at the remark. She was warming up to him. Not

only was he handsome, he was complimentary as well, and she liked the attention.

Lexington could see that he was totally interested in Terra, and that she didn't have a chance at stealing his attention, so she excused herself and walked over to the group of Abercrombie boys. Within minutes, she was standing in the center of the crowd and chatting up the cutest guy in the bunch.

"She's something else," he said, watching her mesmerize the youngster.

"That she is," Terra said, looking at her ego-maniac friend soak up all the attention she was getting.

The bartender kept their glasses full as they traded bits and pieces of their lives. Ironically, they both left out the most important details. Terra didn't mention that her last name was Benson, and Mason failed to mention that he managed a sex club for a living. They had nearly polished off the fifth of vodka, and were feeling no pain. Terra had loosened up considerably, and was now laughing easily at his corny jokes.

"When I was a kid, our apartment was so small that the welcome mat was wall-to-wall carpeting," he said, mimicking Rodney Dangerfield.

"That's too funny," she said, laughing, and slapped his thigh.

A charge ran up Mason's leg at her touch. He put his hand on top of hers and held it in place. She didn't pull away, and he was glad.

Terra glanced down at their hands, and then her eyes traveled up to his crotch area. Her eyes lit up when she saw his full package. His legs were cocked open, giving her a complete view of what he had to offer, and the offering was substantial. She was getting wet just thinking about releasing his captive penis, and riding it up and down. She hadn't had sex in so long that she wondered if her pussy still worked.

Mason saw the look of lust in her eyes and said, "Come on, let's get out of here." He quickly settled the tab, grabbed her hand, and led the way outside. He put one arm over her shoulders and hailed a taxi with the other. While they waited, he whispered another corny joke in her ear, and she broke into a fit of laughter. The combination of the booze and his one-liners had put her totally at ease, and she relaxed back in his arms like they had been dating for years. Once the taxi pulled up to the curb, they hopped inside.

Mason told the driver his address, and then pulled Terra close to him. He searched her eyes for permission to take it to the next level, and they told him to go for it. He leaned in and kissed her deeply, then eased her back on the seat. Mason had tasted her lips; now he wanted to taste her other lips. He quickly unzipped her jeans, pulled them open, and buried his face in her manicured bush. He slipped his tongue in her slit and then sucked her clit.

"Oh, shit." She put her hands on his bald head. "Oh, Baby, yes!"

Mason took a few more sucks, and stopped. He zipped her jeans back and sat her upright like nothing had happened.

"Why'd you stop?" she asked, totally frustrated. "I was just about to cum."

He kissed her neck and inhaled her delicious perfume, which smelled sweet and spicy at the same time. "You smell so good that I could just eat you up."

"Well, why don't you finish the job you started?" she asked, easing closer to him.

"Because I don't want you to cum yet, that was just a little sample." He kissed her again.

Terra squirmed in the seat. She was on fire and his teasing was only making it worse. He had turned her on, and now was making her wait. "Come on, let me have a little more," she said, rubbing his cock. She could feel him getting hard and wanted to suck his dick.

Mason moved her hand and pressed the fabric of the jeans around the outline of his growing erection. "Is this what you want, Baby?"

She looked down and saw that he was at least ten inches. Her mouth watered. "Yes, please let me suck it," she asked again.

"No. You'll have to wait until we get upstairs." Mason knew he was making her crazy, because he was making himself crazy at the same time. He wanted her more than he could say, but there was no time for a backseat fuck, because the taxi was pulling up in front of his building. He paid the driver, got out, and then helped her out. He hugged her tight and pressed his groin into her. "I'm going to love you so good tonight," he whispered in her ear.

"Come on. Let's go upstairs, so you can put your dick where your mouth is." She pulled away and strutted toward the entrance with him following closely behind.

They had barely made it in the front door of his apartment before shoes were kicked off and clothes went flying in the air. Mason pressed her against the wall and kissed her nipples. He then traveled south and finished the clit job that he had started in the taxi.

"That's right, eat that pussy, Baby," she moaned.

Mason loved verbal women. At the coffee shop with her cardigan tied around her neck she looked so prim and proper that he was surprised to hear her dirty talk. "Don't worry, I'ma please the pussy all right," he said between licks.

"And I'm gonna suck all the cum out of your big dick. Now lay me down, so we can sixty-nine, because I'm not into this sixty-eight shit," she demanded.

Mason scooped her in his arms and carried her to the bedroom. He laid her on the comforter and they assumed the position. She scissored her legs around his face while he sucked her clit. She kissed his balls before putting them into her mouth, and after some sensuous sucking, released them to make room for his steel rod.

She tickled the top of his engorged head with her tongue before devouring his entire shaft. A little trick she learned from the good professor.

"Damn, Baby, you got a deep throat."

"I told you I'm going to suck the cum right out of your big dick," she said, coming up for air.

Mason flipped her over and got on top. "Not tonight. Tonight it's all about you," he said, kissing her full on the lips before she could respond. His only desire was to please her in ways she never dreamed about.

Terra spread her legs wide and wrapped them around his back. "I want to feel your dick inside of me right now. Fuck me," she whispered in his ear.

"I'm not going to fuck you." He looked deep into her eyes. "I'm going to make love to you." Mason eased the head of his dick inside, and watched her face respond with pleasure. He slowly entered her and the tightness of her warm pussy turned him on even more than sucking her clit. He increased his pace until they were both riding the same wave. Their bodies melded together like two pieces of molten clay. Though Mason had fucked randomly at the club, this was the first time in a long time that he made love. He knew it was a cliché, but he loved Terra the first time he laid eyes on her. He reached underneath her and held her close with both arms as they came together.

"Wow, that was amazing!" She smiled, still in his arms.

Mason kissed her forehead. "I know. I feel like a new man," he confessed. He turned over to his side, and spooned her. Mason had finally found his anchor, and he wasn't letting go.

He drifted off into a peaceful sleep, and when he woke up in the morning, he was still hugging her. She was comfortable in his arms, which pleased him to no end. He smiled and opened his eyes to see his soul mate, but she was gone, replaced by a down pillow.

He threw the pillow across the bed, got up, and looked in the bathroom, but she wasn't there. He walked into the living room, but no Terra. He peeked in the kitchen, hoping that she was fixing a morning-after breakfast, but the pots were cold and she was nowhere to be found.

"Damn!" He slammed his fists on the slate counter. She was gone without even a good-bye kiss or a note. He didn't have her number and couldn't call information because he didn't even know her last name. "Damn!" he shouted again. In one night, he'd found *and* lost his precious anchor.

13

"MAN, I didn't know you hung out with the rich and famous," Trey said teasingly as soon as Mason picked up the telephone.

Mason had forsaken his morning run and was back underneath the covers. He was still brooding over Terra's unexpected departure and was in no mood for kidding around. "What are you talking about?" he asked dryly.

"I'm talking about you hanging out with Ms. Benson, the hot tobacco heiress. Damn, Dawg, I didn't know you had it like that," Trey said, full of admiration. He'd read about her in *People*, as one of the richest bachelorettes under thirty. Not only was she mega-rich, she was beautiful as well.

"Man, have you been drinking early this morning?" Mason asked, totally clueless as to what Trey was talking about.

"No, I haven't been drinking, but from the looks of this picture, it seems like you and Ms. Benson had tied one on and were feeling no pain."

"What picture? What are you talking about?" Mason asked, getting irritated.

"I take it you haven't read *The Post* yet?"

"No. I'm still in bed," he said lazily.

"Well in that case, let me read you the caption from 'Page Six' 'Ms. Benson's Buffed Beau.' And then it goes on to say—'Terra Benson, the paparazzi-shy tobacco heiress, normally steers clear of the camera, but last night she was seen tumbling out of Pravda at two-thirty A.M. with a no-name stud.'"

Mason shot straight up in bed like a lightning rod. "You've got to be kidding? You mean I'm on 'Page Six' with an heiress?" He was stunned, and slightly pleased at the same time. Though he dated a variety of women, this was the first time his picture had appeared in the paper as someone's "no-name stud." Being featured on "Page Six" was an unofficial honor, unless it was bad press. But being affiliated with an heiress was indeed a high honor.

"No, I'm not kidding, and yes you're on 'Page Six'. And considering the fact that she's rarely photographed, I wouldn't be surprised if the photographer sells this picture to the tabloids."

"Let's hope not; being in *The Post* is one thing, but I'd hate to have my mug in those cheesy papers near the supermarket checkout lines. So her last name is Benson?" Mason said, thinking out loud.

"Man, you mean to tell me you didn't know that you were hanging out with one of the most eligible heiresses in the world? How did you meet her anyway? From what I've read, she's extremely private and hates to be photographed," Trey said, trying to get the inside scoop.

"I literally bumped into her at Borders, and last night we were both coincidently at Pravda. I bought her and her friend a bottle service, and the next thing you know, she and I are drinking and talking like old friends, and—"

"And you got her drunk, took her home, and fucked her brains out," Trey interrupted, infusing his own version of the story.

"Man, it wasn't like that at all . . . well, it was like that, but"—Mason took a deep breath—"I think I'm in love with her," he admitted rather sheepishly.

"You mean you're in love with the punnay." Trey had never known Mason to have a serious girlfriend, only random booty calls.

"Naw, Man, this girl is different. The first time I laid eyes on her, I knew she was something special," Mason said with a smile in his voice.

"She's something special, all right. A billion dollars' worth of special. Do you realize what her family is worth? She comes from old money, and we both know that old money lasts for generations and generations, unlike new money, that's usually squandered by the first generation."

"Man, I don't care about her money. When I met her last night, she told me that she was a struggling actress, and I'm good with that," Mason said.

"She's a struggling actress with a seven- or eight-figure trust fund, so I just bet you're good with that!" Trey chuckled.

"I told you I don't care about her family's money. I would love her if she was waiting tables at a diner for minimum wage. I may not be worth a billion dollars, but I'm not hurting financially either. I've saved a nice little nest egg, enough to support a family when the time is right."

Trey had never heard Mason speak so passionately about anyone before, and was beginning to believe him. "Since you're so in love, when's your next date with Ms. Benson?"

"Your guess is as good as mine," he said, slumping back on the headboard.

"Now I'm confused. The way you were talking, I thought you'd be running down to Tiffany's for a five-carat engagement ring." He laughed.

"I'm glad you think my love life is a joke. If you must know, she left my apartment this morning before I woke up, without leaving her number."

"Oh, no, she crept out on you? I thought only men snuck out on the sly before the light of day, without saying good-bye or leaving a note. You have to admit the girl's got game," Trey said, sounding impressed.

"Believe it or not, for once in my life, I don't want to play any games. I'm ready for a relationship, and she's 'the one.'"

" 'The one'? Are you sure?" Trey asked, knowing that when a man used that phrase it meant a marriage proposal wasn't too far behind.

"Yep, she's 'the one.' Now all I have to do is find her and convince her to marry me and have my babies." He chuckled, but was serious nonetheless. Thinking that Terra might be at Borders, Mason said abruptly, "Look, Man, I gotta go. Talk to you later."

"Okay, see you in the papers," Trey ribbed him once again before hanging up.

Mason showered and shaved quickly. He put on a fresh pair of jeans and a long-sleeved Juicy Couture T-shirt. Instead of his old beat-up running shoes, he wore a pair of black and tan Pumas. He wanted to look casually clean, just in case Terra was in Borders.

He was so excited that he nearly ran to the bookstore and into the café. He scanned the small room, but she wasn't there. He ordered his usual, and sat at a corner table that faced the doorway. His eyes were peeled to the entrance as he watched people come and go, but no Terra.

TERRA SAT IN her bed with the trades spread across the damask duvet, but instead of reading the latest industry news, she was staring at the picture of herself and Mason on *Page Six*. In the photograph, they were both laughing (probably at one of his jokes), his arm was comfortably around her shoulders, and they appeared to be slightly inebriated. It surely didn't look like they had met only hours before the picture was snapped. Terra had felt so comfortable with Mason that she let her guard down, and was unaware of her surroundings once they went outside. Normally she was cautious and wore over-sized sunglasses to help conceal her face just in case there were photographers lurking about. But last night, all of her inhibitions were cast aside. It was a combination of the vodka and Mason's easygoing personality that had her tipsy, and she totally forgot about shielding her identity from the paparazzi.

As she was reading the caption for the umpteenth time, the telephone rang. "Hello?" she asked skeptically, hoping it wasn't her parents calling about her début on "Page Six."

"I was wondering where you had disappeared to last night, but after seeing *The Post* this morning, I'm guessing you spent the night at his place," Lexi said as soon as Terra picked up the phone.

"Whatever happened to 'Good morning'?" Terra asked sarcastically. She wasn't ready to talk about her wild night with Mason. She'd planned on letting that be her little secret, but now that their picture was splashed across the paper for the world to see, she had no choice but to tell Lexi the story.

"From the looks of this picture, I'd say you had a good night. So tell me everything, and don't spare any of the juicy details. Do his lips taste as good as they look?" Lexi asked, getting right down to the nitty-gritty.

Terra sighed as if reliving the moment when his lips first touched hers. "Better. Girl, I hadn't planned on sleeping with him, but we were laughing and drinking and the next thing you know—"

"You were riding his soul pole." Lexi laughed.

"Trust me, that totally wasn't the plan, but when I peeked at his package when we were sitting at the bar, I just couldn't resist. I hadn't had sex since David left for California over a year ago, and I was long overdue."

"I thought you didn't do one-night stands," Lexi said, knowing how cautious Terra could be about protecting her identity.

"I normally don't, but it's not like he was a total stranger. I mean, I have seen him a few times at Borders," she said, trying to redeem herself.

"So . . . was he any good?"

"Lexi, Lexi, Lexi." Terra fanned the newspaper across her face. "Good isn't even the word. He was awesome!"

"Awesome? That's a strong adjective. I'm sure you're exaggerating since you haven't had sex in so long," she said, discounting Terra's claim. Lexi was slightly jealous. She had wanted to fuck Mason the second she saw him across the room, but he only had eyes for Terra. After he dismissed her, she silently cursed him, wishing that he had a small prick and no skills.

"I'm not exaggerating in the least. From the taxi ride to his apartment, we couldn't keep our hands off of each other. He even went down on me in the back of the cab. I've never had sex in the backseat of a car before and the thought of the driver hearing us moan really turned me on." Terra wedged a pillow between her legs, wishing it were Mason's dick. Just talking about him was making her moist, and she wanted to go back to his apartment and finish where they had left off, but it wasn't in the cards.

"Okay, I get the picture." Lexi didn't want to hear any more, because secretly she wished that Mason were eating her out in the back of a taxi instead of her friend. "What about Sage?" Lexi asked, reminding Terra about her plan of seduction.

"Oh, yeah." Terra had momentarily forgotten about Sage and the movie studio. She was thinking about fucking Mason again, instead of focusing on her scheme to win Sage over. "I surely hope he hasn't read *The Post* this morning, because from the looks of this picture Mason and I seem as if we're headed straight for the bedroom," Terra said, glancing at the photo one more time.

"What if he has? Then what are you going to do?"

"I'll just say that you and I were out with a few friends and that picture was part of a group shot, edited down to look like I was on a date. Sage knows the business and how photographers manipulate pictures to their advantage," Terra said. Now that she had a logical explanation, she felt better about being outed on *Page Six*.

"Okay, that takes care of the picture, but what are you going to do about Mason? Are you going to see him again?"

"No, that was a one-night affair, and I've got to stay focused," Terra said, wedging the pillow deeper between her legs. Her mind was saying forget about him, but her body wanted more of his tongue, fingers, and most of all his big, beautiful dick. He had made love to her so good that she was craving him all over again, but he was one addiction that she couldn't afford.

14

"ROY, THANKS for coming over straight from the airport," Sage said, shaking his hand and inviting the architect into his office.

After their last conversation, when Roy informed Sage that the building couldn't accommodate four full-sized studios, Sage was extremely curt and practically hung up in the man's face. Once he calmed down, Sage realized that hiring another architectural firm wasn't the answer—Roy Snyderman was the best—so he swallowed his attitude and called Roy in for a meeting.

"You're welcome," he said, shaking Sage's hand in return. "I've figured out a solution to the problem," Roy said, sitting at the mini conference table opposite Sage's desk and unrolling a set of floor plans.

"That's good to hear. Let's see what you have," Sage said, pulling up a chair.

"We were able to work around the two structural pillars without compromising the roof. So instead of two sets, we're able to build three," he said, pointing to the outline of the proposed sets.

Sage leaned in and looked at the drawings; though it wasn't the original plan for the soundstage, he was pleased with the new drawings. He had the resources to scrap the plans and start from scratch, but he wanted to stay on schedule. Though his father was retired, Sage knew that his old man kept abreast of what was happening with the business, and he didn't want to give his father any cause for concern. "Since this is a new layout, are we going to have to get these plans approved by the city?"

"If you approve of this layout, then I'll call in a few favors and have them rushed through. Since we're not adding onto the square footage of the building, it shouldn't be a problem."

"I definitely approve. Thanks so much for all of your help; I really appreciate it. I apologize for blowing up last time, but this studio is my baby, and I want it to be perfect," Sage said sincerely. His mother had always taught him that you get more flies with honey than with vinegar, and she was right.

"I totally understand." Roy began rerolling the drawings. "I'll have the originals messengered down to City Hall. We shouldn't be more than a week behind schedule, which isn't bad at all," he said, looking at Sage for his reaction.

"A week I can live with." Sage smiled. "Do you have time for a drink? I feel like celebrating."

"Sure, I know this great martini bar on Sixty-eighth between Lex and Park."

"Great, let me call for my driver," Sage said, reaching for the phone.

"Don't bother. My car is already downstairs, and I'll drop you off afterward," Roy offered.

"Sounds good." Sage put on his suit jacket that was hanging behind the door, straightened his tie, and they headed out of the office.

The R Lounge was located in the basement of a brownstone building. With only a small bronze plaque with the name etched on it, the bar was easy to miss.

"How did you find this place? It's so unassuming, I would have walked right past without noticing it existed."

"I own the building and the bar. I purposely designed the space to be inconspicuous. I wanted a spot where I could feel comfortable being myself, and have great drinks in a relaxing environment," Roy said, opening the door to the lounge.

From the look of the residential exterior, Sage expected the bar to look like a cozy living room with sofas and a fireplace, but the interior was sleek. A long chrome bar expanded the length of the room, and was illuminated from underneath with indigo lights. Instead of down-filled couches, black leather cubes served as additional seating, opposite the bar stools. The wall facing the bar was mirrored, giving the narrow space depth. Hypnotic groove music played in the background, as hip-looking patrons sipped martinis and chatted among one another. Roy waved to a few people as they made their way to the bar.

"Hey there, Roy, long time, no see," the bartender said.

"I've been out of the country, but I'm back now and ready for one of your concoctions. What are you shaking up tonight?"

Stan was one of the best mixologists in the city and made daily drink specials from unique ingredients. "A Velvet Cane, made with 10 Cane Rum and Moët White Star poured over a raw sugar cube. You want to try one?"

"Make it two," Sage said. As he waited for Stan to mix their drinks, he checked out the scene. Beautiful women of varying shapes and sizes sat together talking, while the men—who were equally as attractive—looked on from afar. As Sage was glancing around, he noticed a gorgeous redhead with a Rene Russo face and a killer Pamela Anderson body walk into the bar. She was short, but was packaged nicely. The tight, multicolored wrap dress she wore hugged every curve of her body, and the deep V-neckline showcased her double Ds.

Since Roy seemed to know quite a few people in the place, Sage whispered, "Who is that?"

"Trouble." He smirked.

She walked between Sage and Roy, ran her hand up Roy's arm, and said, "Hey, Baby, you're looking exceptionally good this evening. I haven't seen you around in a while, where have you been?"

Roy was in his mid-forties, but looked every bit of thirty-five. He worked out regularly resulting in a taut midsection, firm shoulders, and buns of steel. He had a perpetual tan that highlighted his hazel eyes. Roy's style was impeccable. With his London office within walking distance of Bond Street and Savile Row, he had his suits tailor-made. His casual clothes came from Canali, Pellini, and Lanvin, and were in muted tones of tan, gray, and black. "Hey, Babe." He kissed her on the lips. "I've been in London."

"I'm glad you're back," she said, moving her body closer to his and returning his kiss.

It was obvious these two were more than friends. Sage only knew Roy on a professional basis, and didn't know if he was in a committed relationship or not. Seeing them in a lip lock made Sage feel like an unwanted third wheel. "Well, it looks like you guys want to be alone," he said, finishing his drink. "Roy, call me once the plans are approved," he said, and started to walk away.

"Wait a minute." She touched Sage's arm. "Who said we want to be alone?"

"I don't want to intrude." He put his empty glass on the bar.

"It's no intrusion, is it, Roy?" She looked up at him for validation.

"Definitely not." He turned to the bartender and ordered another round. "Sage, this is Lena," he said, finally making an introduction.

She turned her body toward Sage, extended her hand, and looked him up and down. "Nice to meet you." She smiled.

He glanced down and couldn't help but stare into her cleavage. The low-cut dress barely covered her enlarged breasts, and he could see the top of her pink areolas. "Nice to meet you too," he said, darting his eyes from her breasts to her face.

Lena noticed Sage practically drooling at her titties, and smiled slyly. "Just so you know, they're real." She turned to Roy. "Aren't they, Baby?"

"Oh, yeah. One hundred percent." He grabbed her by the waist and pulled her in front of him so that her ass was against his groin.

Sage watched as she discreetly began grinding into Roy's cock. They were making him horny, and he decided to go home and call Missy for some phone boning. "It was nice meeting you, Lena, but I really have to go."

"We're leaving too." She grabbed Roy's hand. "And you're coming with us." She reached out for Sage's hand. Standing between the two handsome men, and holding each one by the hand, Lena smiled. "Now this is what I call a dynamic duo." Lena turned to the bartender. "Stan, cancel that round."

Sage was curious as to where they were headed, but decided to go with the flow and not ruin the mood with too many questions.

Lena dropped both of their hands and led the way through the lounge and out the door with Roy and Sage following closely behind. Outside, she turned right and walked up a flight of steps to the first floor of the brownstone. She unlocked the door and stood to the side, inviting them into the apartment.

Lena shut the door, walked over to the mantel, and lit a few votive candles. Sage looked around the room, which was sparsely furnished with a love seat and end table near the huge bay window and a few unopened boxes wedged in one corner. There were no pictures on the walls, and the hardwood floors were bare.

From the looks of the apartment, he assumed that she'd recently moved in.

After lighting the candles, Lena turned on the stereo and a soft, sexy French ballet began to play. She sauntered into the middle of the living room—which without much furniture looked like a dance floor—and began a slow striptease to the music. She unwrapped the tie around her waist that held her wrap dress together, causing the fabric to flow open, exposing her naked body.

Sage watched as she swayed to the music and her overripe boobs swung from side to side. Unlike surgically enhanced breasts that barely moved, hers were jiggling all over the place. His mouth began to salivate at the thought of sucking on her nipples, and he licked his lips.

She let the dress drop to the floor and danced over to Roy, who was also licking his lips. "Let's show your friend how I like my tits sucked."

He didn't say a word, just got on his knees and pulled her toward him, so that her nipples were directly on his lips. He stuck out his tongue and trailed the outline of her areola, before sucking her right nipple, and then the left.

Sage's dick was rising into an erection as he watched Roy feast from titty to titty. He unbuckled his belt, slipped his hand into his pants, and began stroking himself while watching his own private porn show.

Lena looked over and saw him masturbating. "Come over here, Baby, and let me taste you."

Sage took off his pants and walked over with his erection in hand. He stood on the side of Lena. She turned her head, leaned down, took his dick in her mouth, and began sucking him off. "Oh, yeah, that feels so good," he said, closing his eyes.

"You like it, Baby?" she whispered.

"Oh, yeah, don't stop," he said with his eyes still closed and on the verge of cumming. She was sucking him so good that he was ready to explode. Sage opened his eyes, so he could see his cum shoot down her throat, and froze.

"What's wrong, Baby? Isn't Roy sucking you good enough?" Lena asked.

Sage stared in shock. He had been in some freaky situations before, and it was rare that anything rendered him speechless, but for the moment he was at a loss for words. He had no idea that Roy was into men. Sage could usually spot a man on the DL, because there was something in their eyes that gave away their dirty little secret, but Sage had never seen that look of lust in Roy's eyes, until now. Roy was looking up at him for his reaction, while he deep-throated him. Roy had gone from sucking Lena's tits to sucking Sage's cock.

"He's doing better than good," Sage said, finally finding his voice. He smiled slyly, and rammed his dick farther down Roy's throat.

It was common knowledge that Sage was a metrosexual, but very few knew that he was bisexual as well. Sage didn't consider himself on the DL, because he always pitched and never received, so as far as he was concerned, he wasn't gay, he was just freaky and if a man wanted to suck his dick, he had no objections as long as he wasn't expected to return the favor.

Lena played with her pussy as she watched Sage cum in Roy's mouth. She was the ultimate fag-hag, and got off on seeing men-on-men action. "Now that you got your rocks off," she said to Sage, "it's my turn. Come on, Roy, give me some of that cock of yours."

Roy loved pleasing both men and women, and could easily flip from one to the other without hesitation. After sucking Sage off, his dick was aching for some release of its own, so he ripped off his clothes and eased Lena down on the floor. He spread her legs open and eased in between them. He slipped his dick inside of her wet opening and began humping and grinding.

While they were in the throes of ecstasy, Sage put his pants back on and tipped out the door, leaving them alone to handle their business. His dick was satisfied; now all he wanted to do was go home, take a nice long bath, have a bite to eat, and relive his unexpected ménage à trois.

15

IT HAD been two days since his debut on *Page Six*, and Mason still hadn't seen or heard from Terra. Now that he knew her first and last name, he Googled her in the hopes of getting her phone number and address, but no personal information appeared after he entered her name. He should have known that someone of her stature would have their most private information blocked from the general public. He was desperate to know more about her, so he read every article that had ever been printed about the young heiress. He learned that she was an only child and the sole heir to the Benson Tobacco fortune, a fortune worth well over a billion dollars. There weren't many photos, but there were some pictures of her at charity functions, and photographs of herself and her parents at their beachfront estate in the Hamptons. He even found some of her as a child taking riding lessons, but no photos of her linked romantically with anyone. Most heiresses of her stature dated shipping tycoons and partied with A-list movie stars, but the only mention of a love connection was her friendship with Sage Hirschfield. One article suggested that they might be more than just friends, and had pictures of them dining at the Spice Market. Mason looked closely at the snapshot, and had to admit that they did look chummy sitting together at a cozy booth. He remembered her calling Sage, the first day he met her, and didn't know if they were involved. If they were, it couldn't be too serious since she fucked him for hours on end the other night. He didn't care if Terra was involved with Sage; all he cared about was finding her, and this time he wouldn't let go. He'd even gone back to Pravda on the off chance that she would be sitting at the bar sipping a cocktail, but of course she wasn't there.

Terra didn't have his cell or home number, so he didn't expect a call, but she knew where he lived and could have easily dropped a note off with the doorman. He staked out Borders after his morning run, hoping to find Ms. Benson, but she was nowhere in sight. Short of hiring a private investigator to find his anchor, Mason didn't know what to do, so he went home to get ready for work.

"How was your run, Mr. Anthony?" Frank, the doorman, asked.

"It was good. Got to keep the heart rate up so I can stay forever young." He grinned.

"I started working out myself." Frank patted his fat belly. "Gotta get this stomach down." He reached underneath the desk, took out a pink letter-sized envelope, and handed it to Mason. "This came for you while you were out jogging."

Mason looked at the script and didn't recognize the handwriting. He turned the envelope over, but there wasn't a return address on the back, only his name written in black ink on the front. "Did this come by messenger service?" he asked, since there was no postmark or any other discerning marks.

"No, a beautiful young lady dropped it off about five minutes after you left."

Mason knew instantly that it was from Terra. "Did she say

anything?" he asked eagerly, thirsty for any information about his dream girl.

"She just said to give you the envelope the minute you walked through the door. She thanked me, and then left." Frank whistled softly. "What a looker! You sure know how to pick 'em."

"Yeah, she's a beautiful lady." Mason smiled proudly, like she was already his woman. He then raced through the lobby and upstairs so he could read his love letter in private. He couldn't wait to see what Terra had to say. It was probably an invitation to join her for dinner *and* dessert. Earlier he was thinking that she could have dropped her information off with the doorman, and as luck would have it, she did.

The second he stepped inside the apartment and closed the door, he put the envelope up to his nose and sniffed, hoping to smell the intoxicating perfume that tickled his nose the other night, but the scent was fresh and flowery, unlike hers. He ripped open the seal nonetheless, took out the note, and read it:

Hey Handsome,

Saw your face on Page Six. I see you still look as good as you did in college. Even better, I might add. I would love to catch up and talk about old times. Here's my card with my cell number. Looking forward to hearing from you soon.

Always,

R.S.

Mason reread the note again. He couldn't believe his eyes. This was the last person he wanted to hear from. He didn't even look at the number, just ripped the card to pieces, balled up the note, and tossed them both in the trash. He had no intention of reconnecting with the past. He'd spent years distancing himself from unsavory memories, and had done a good job, until now. His college days were far behind him, and he planned to keep it that way.

TERRA HADN'T heard from Sage in over a week, and was getting paranoid. Maybe he had seen her picture on "Page Six," and assumed that she was dating Mason, or maybe he was interested in someone else now. She didn't want to come right out and ask him if he'd seen the picture, just in case he hadn't, so she decided to call and ask about his father instead, and during the conversation she would hint around to find out exactly what he knew.

"Hey there, stranger, I was calling to ask how your dad is feeling," she said after his secretary put her through to his private line.

"Hey, yourself. He's doing fine," Sage answered, totally forgetting his lie.

"So why was he taken to the emergency room?" she asked with concern in her voice.

As soon as she mentioned "emergency room," he remembered running out on her at dinner claiming that his dad had been rushed to the hospital. "Uh, he had a mild case of food poisoning," he said.

"I'm glad it wasn't anything serious." Terra genuinely liked Mr. Hirschfield, and was relieved to hear that it was something minor.

"Me too. He's fully recovered now and back to his old self. So, where have you been hiding?" he asked, quickly changing the subject.

From that comment, Terra assumed that he hadn't seen her picture plastered on "Page Six," but she still wasn't sure, so she decided to probe. "I haven't been hiding. I've been out and about. What about you? What have you been up to?"

"Nothing much. Just working like an indentured servant." He chuckled.

"Oh, poor thing. With all that work, I'm sure you don't even have time to read the paper or party," she said, continuing her fishing expedition.

"You're right. I barely have time to read the status reports that come across my desk, let alone the newspaper. Well, I take that back. I do read *The Wall Street Journal* and *The Times* every morning, but the other papers just get chucked in the garbage."

This was just what Terra wanted to hear, and she silently breathed a sigh of relief. But the relief was short-lived, because if he hadn't seen the picture, why hadn't he called her? she wondered. Terra dismissed the notion of him dating someone else and decided to focus on her goal. "I have a great idea. Come over to my place after work, and I'll call my personal masseuse and have her ease your tired muscles. Doesn't that sound heavenly?"

"Yes, that does sound great, but I can't. I'm up to my eyeballs in work. How about a rain check?" he asked, sounding distracted.

She didn't expect him to say that. Normally, he would have leaped at the chance to be with her. The tables had suddenly shifted, and now she was the one hunting Sage down for a date instead of the other way around. "Okay, just say the word and my masseuse is all yours," she said, trying to hide her disappointment.

"I'll give you a call next week and we can set something up. I hate to run, but I'm late for a meeting," he said, rushing her off the telephone.

Terra barely got out the word "good-bye," before she heard the dial tone in her ear. She hung up the phone and walked over to the living-room picture window that overlooked the Hudson River. As she gazed into the moving body of water, she began to assess the situation. *He must be getting laid. Otherwise he'd be trying to get in my panties, like so many times before,* she thought. She knew men, and if they were not pressing you for sex, that was only because they were getting it from someone else. And the way Sage was acting, all cool and collected, she had no doubt that he was being sexed up by somebody. Her seduction scheme was losing steam faster than a vintage locomotive, and she needed to hatch plan B, before he cast another actress as the lead in his first production. Terra paced back and forth trying to think of another angle, but she was fresh out of ideas. Frustrated, she moped over to the sofa and plopped down. As she was racking her brain for ideas, the telephone rang.

"Hello?" she said dryly.

"Hey, Girl. What's wrong with you?" Lexi asked, picking up on the sour tone.

"I just hung up with Sage, and he could care less about seeing me. I invited him over tonight for a massage, and he turned me down flat, then said that he would call me next week!" she shrieked into the receiver. "Can you believe that? He's never declined an opportunity to see me."

"Maybe he saw the picture of you on 'Page Six,' and thinks that you're involved with Mason," Lexi said.

"No, he didn't. I hinted around and he said that he only reads *The Times* and *The Journal*. I honestly think that he just isn't interested anymore," she said, sounding like a wounded puppy.

"Well, fuck him. It's not like he's the only movie producer in the world. Why don't you have your agent line up a few screen tests? That way you won't have to depend on Sage for your big break," Lexi suggested.

"Yeah, I could do that, but it'll be much easier to deal with Sage. At least he knows me and I wouldn't have to compete with other actresses for the best role. I just have to find another approach, because obviously the seduction routine isn't working. Lexi, you've got to help me come up with a new plan of attack," she said, sounding desperate.

"Don't worry, between the two of us we'll think of something clever. But in the meantime, I know just what you need to lift your spirits." In contrast to Terra's somber mood, Lexi's was bright and bubbly. She'd found the perfect stress-buster and couldn't wait to tell Terra all about it.

"I'm not in the mood for shopping," Terra said, knowing that Lexi's ultimate cure-all was a romp down Fifth Avenue.

"Neither am I. What I have in mind is so much better than shopping! You won't believe what I've discovered," she said, suddenly sounding mysterious.

"What?" Terra asked unenthusiastically.

"A club exclusively for women!" she said excitedly, like she'd just discovered the cure to some dreaded disease.

"I don't feel like working out either," Terra said, misinterpreting what Lexi was saying.

"Good, because I'm not talking about a gym. This club is called the Black Door and it's an erotic playground just for women. Men can't be members, they can only work there," she said, giving Terra the lowdown.

"What? Are you kidding? How did you find out about this place?" Terra asked, with her mood gradually lifting.

"Last week when I was at Barneys, I ran into an old classmate from NYU, who was a party promoter back in school. Between picking out Marc Jacobs bags, I asked her if there were any new hot clubs not on the radar yet, and she gave me the scoop about the Black Door. She said it's for members only and is off the chain. She told me that there are several rooms where you can get your freak on, dance, play pool, or eat aphrodisiacs. So put your party shoes on, because we're going to check out every single room tonight!" Lexi said excitedly, sounding like a kid who had just discovered a new candy.

"How are we going to the club if it's for members only?"

"Because I joined a few days ago, that's how!" She smiled into the receiver, and then went on to explain. "I met with the owner, Trey Curtis, who is fine as hell, I might add, at the main club uptown, and after going through an extensive interview process, he approved my membership and personally designed a mask for me."

Terra had never heard of anything like this and was full of questions. "What's the mask for?"

"Oh, I forgot to tell you, all the members and the servers wear masks, so you're free to get your freak on without anyone knowing your true identity."

"I like the sound of that, but what about me? I'm not a member, so how am I supposed to get into the club?" Hearing about the details of the Black Door had Terra totally intrigued and she'd forgotten about her dilemma with Sage.

"I borrowed my friend's mask for the evening, and if you like what you see tonight, then you can join too."

"Sounds like a plan." Terra's dark mood was completely lifted now, and she was eager to experience something different. Professor Langston had taught her in acting class to always seek out new adventures and store them in your memory bank to use when needed. "Instead of having Leroy drive us, let's take a taxi. I don't want him in my business."

"Since I live on the way, why don't you pick me up in an hour?"

"Okay, see you then," Terra said, and hung up.

Terra was so caught up in the excitement of hearing about such a decadent club that she agreed to go without giving it a second thought. But now that she had gotten off the phone and had a minute to digest all the information, she began to feel a bit hesitant. What if a nosy photographer snapped her picture going into or coming out of the club? It was one thing being seen leaving a lounge, but the press would have a field day if they caught wind of her partying at a place like the Black Door. She picked up the phone to call Lexi back, and tell her that she wasn't going, but hung up before completing the call. With a mask concealing her identity, she rationalized that even if photographers were lurking around, they wouldn't have a clue that she was the woman behind the mask. Besides, checking out the club would take her mind off of Sage, and she definitely needed a momentary distraction.

Terra went into her bedroom closet to decide what to wear. Since they were going to a sex club, she chose a black leather halter top with matching miniskirt, fishnets, and a pair of red four-inch Rene Caovilla sandals with a faceted jeweled ankle strap. Instead of wearing her hair curly, she blew it straight for that long flowing look. She sprayed her neck and wrists with L'Heure Magique before putting on a white Andrew Marc raincoat to conceal her outfit from the nosy doorman, and headed out the door.

Lexi was waiting outside of her building when the taxi pulled up. She was also wearing a trench coat, and laughed once she got inside the cab and saw Terra's. "I see great minds think alike."

"I didn't feel like dealing with a million and two questions from my doorman. He's used to seeing me suited up. Probably thinks I'm some type of prude and I want to keep it that way. The last thing I need is for him to call one of those tabloids and tell them that Terra Benson is hooking at night." She'd read too many articles about a celebrity assistant or someone close to their camp selling stories and pictures for thousands of dollars to the rags. Terra didn't think her doorman would betray her privacy, but it paid to be cautious nonetheless.

"You don't look like a ho." Lexi surveyed her outfit. "Well, maybe a little." She laughed.

"Who you calling a ho? Let's see what you have on."

Lexi untied her belt, revealing a hot pink, see-through blouse, but you couldn't see her nipples because she wore pink pasties to conceal her breasts. Her pants were crocheted, revealing her skin through the pink yarn. And she had on a pair of silver Giuseppe Zanotti jeweled T-strap sandals to complete the outfit. "Thought I'd wear pink to match my mask," she said, removing a pink mask with silver rhinestones around the eyes from a brown paper bag.

"Wow, that's beautiful," Terra said, touching the delicate half mask. "Where's mine?"

Lexi then took out a burnt orange mask covered with multicolored faceted stones and handed it to Terra. "Here, and be careful because I have to return it tomorrow."

"No problem," she said, tying the mask around her eyes. Terra took out her compact and looked in the mirror. "This is so exciting. You can't even tell it's me," she said after seeing her reflection.

"I know. It feels like we're going to a masquerade ball, except instead of an engraved invitation, you need a password to get in. Your password is 'Unadulterated Lust,' and mine is 'Lick My Clit,' " Lexi said, securing her mask.

"I like your password better. Mine is a little tame."

"Well, if you decide to become a member, you can choose your own password. One more thing, there's a greeter to welcome us before we enter the club."

"A greeter? You mean like a welcoming committee?" Terra asked.

"Not exactly." Lexi raised her eyebrows. "Actually, it's only one man, and his job is to get you all juiced up and ready for the club," Lexi said, taking a tube of pink lipstick out of her purse and applying a layer.

"What do you mean 'all juiced up'?"

"I mean he grabs you from behind, rubs your ass, and if you're willing, massages your clit until you're on the verge of climaxing," Lexi said, closing her eyes for a second, remembering her last encounter with the greeter.

The expression on Terra's face registered shock; this club was sounding more and more seductive by the second. "Are you serious?"

"As serious as Dick Cheney at a gay rally." She laughed.

On the way downtown, Lexi told Terra about the various chambers and what to expect so she wouldn't be shocked by some of the lewd activities. And just as she finished her mini tutorial, the taxi was pulling up in front of a nondescript building in the Meat-Packing District.

Terra got out of the taxi, looked at the building, and was unimpressed by the warehouselike structure whose only discerning feature was a black metal door. From the description of the club that Lexi had painted, she expected to see a renovated facade like most of the other buildings in the area. "This is it?" she said, turning up her lip.

"I know it doesn't look like much on the outside, but just wait until we get upstairs, and you'll see what I'm talking about," Lexi said, leading the way to the front door.

Lexi pressed the tiny bell to the right and a man with a menacing-looking face slid open a small window and asked for their passwords before opening the Black Door. He then took them up in the freight elevator to meet the "greeter."

Gee did exactly what Lexi had said, only Terra didn't let him massage her clit, even though deep down inside she really wanted him to; but that was a little too personal for her. She hadn't had sex since Mason and though it had been only a week, she was horny as hell. Professor Langston had unleashed a desire in her that she never knew existed, and after he left, she had put her libido on ice and concentrated on graduating. Mason had thawed her sexual drive, and now it was in overdrive.

After their warm welcome, Lexi and Terra checked their coats and went into the Disco where Gloria Gaynor was belting out "I Will Survive" over the loudspeakers as strobe lights flashed on the gyrating bodies on the dance floor. They wormed their way to the middle of the crowd and as the song blended into The Weather Girls' "It's Raining Men," two servers began dancing along with them.

Terra's dance partner pulled her close and quickly turned her around so that her butt was directly in front of his cock. He held her by the waist while grinding into her ass. She could feel his dick harden with every beat of the music and grooved in time to his movements.

"You're making me so hard that I want to fuck you right here on the dance floor," he said, reaching underneath her skirt and rubbing his hands between her thighs.

Terra was horny, but she wasn't that horny. She wanted to get laid, but not with a random stud in the middle of a crowd. "No thanks," she said, wiggling out of his embrace and dancing away.

Lexi noticed Terra leaving, and asked over the music, "Where're you going?"

"To check out the rest of the club," she said, making her way to the exit.

"Hold on. I'm coming with you," Lexi said, also dancing away from her partner.

The hallway outside of the Disco was painted midnight blue, and was lit by dim, overhead pin lights. Terra could barely see where she was walking, so she followed Lexi, who knew the lay of the land. As they continued down the darkened corridor, Terra could smell the enticing aroma of chocolate, and she inhaled to get a better whiff.

"Hmm, what smells so good? Is there a bakery here?" she asked Lexi.

"No, that would be the Chocolate Chamber. Come on; let's see what's cooking."

Terra couldn't believe her eyes. Inside were two women, standing in the middle of the floor buck naked, getting their bodies painted with melted chocolate by two servers. A third woman was lying on a chaise lounge with her legs spread-eagle, and a server was licking chocolate off of her clit. "This sure isn't Willy Wonka's Chocolate Factory," she mused.

"No, it's better," Lexi said, walking over to a server who was standing behind a glass display case full of assorted chocolates. "I'm in the mood for white chocolate," she said, pointing to a block of white confection.

"You're not going to have your body painted are you?" Terra whispered in her ear, so the server wouldn't hear.

"Why not? I hate to admit it, but I haven't been laid in months, and my clit needs a little stimulation. I'm tired of turning myself on with my vibrator. Now that I'm here, I want him"—she pointed to a server with rippling muscles underneath alabaster skin and a long ponytail—"to play with Ms. Kitty."

Terra loved her friend dearly, but couldn't imagine watching Lexi get fucked by a Fabio look-alike. "Okay, girl, get your freak on. I'm leaving."

"You're going home already? We just got here."

"No, I'm not going home just yet. I think I'll stop by Hotel Gansevoort for a nightcap. I need a drink to help me process everything I've seen tonight." Terra wasn't a prude by any means. She just wasn't ready for communal sex. A one-night stand she could deal with, but making love in front of strangers was a little too freaky for her tastes.

"Okay, I'll talk to you later," Lexi said, turning back to the server, who was heating her chocolate selection over a double boiler.

Terra made her way back to the lobby, got her coat, and went down in the freight elevator. Once she exited the building, she took the mask off and tucked it in her purse. As she walked the short block over to Hotel Gansevoort, she was totally unaware that she was being followed.

17

SAGE WAS having one of those days from hell. His secretary had called in sick (which was rare) and the temp that the agency sent over was beyond incompetent. She didn't know how to make a decent pot of coffee, so he sent her across the street to Starbucks for a double espresso with low-fat milk, but she came back with a cappuccino with heavy cream instead. And every time she tried to transfer a call to his office, she'd disconnect the caller, and if that wasn't bad enough, she must have been dyslexic because she kept transposing telephone numbers on his messages, so he couldn't even return calls. He was accustomed to Pearl, who'd been with the company since he was a little boy. Having been his father's longtime secretary she was the epitome of efficiency. Pearl arrived at the office before he did, and had his daily itinerary typed and on his desk when he got there. The temp didn't have a clue how to pull up his schedule on the computer, so he had to do her work as well as his, and was getting more frustrated as the day went on.

Sage thought about calling the agency to get a replacement, but he didn't want to chance getting another nincompoop. He made a note for Pearl to change agencies, because clearly this one didn't screen their applicants properly.

"Uh, excuse me, but there's a Ms. Walker on the phone," the temp said, peeking her head through his office door.

"Put her through. On second thought, I'll answer the call at your desk instead," he said, remembering that the girl couldn't transfer calls.

Sage walked out to the secretary's desk, picked up the phone, and said in his most professional voice, "Sage Hirschfield speaking."

"My, my, don't you sound like the Big Kahuna," Missy teased.

"Good afternoon, Ms. Walker, how may I help you?" he asked, ignoring her comment, knowing the temp was standing right over his shoulder and listening to every word he was saying.

"You can help yourself to some good loving," she said suggestively.

"Actually, I was thinking along those same lines. How's six o'clock?"

"Six is perfect. Bring both of your appetites because I'm cooking dinner, and after you eat, you're going to fuck my brains out. See you later, lover," she said, and hung up.

It was four-thirty, and Sage decided not to prolong the agony any longer. "There's no need for you to stay until six. You can leave now," he said to the temp.

"Leave now? But my agency said this assignment wasn't over until six o'clock. If I leave now, I won't get no overtime on my check, and I need the overtime," she said, looking like she was on the verge of tears.

"Don't worry, you'll get paid for a full day. Put your out time as seven o'clock and I'll sign your timesheet," Sage said. He was willing to do just about anything to get this girl out of his office.

"Oh, wow! Thanks, Mr. Hirschfield," she said, smiling from ear to ear.

Once she was gone, Sage went into his private bathroom to freshen up, and then headed out the door and over to Missy's apartment.

"Come here, Girl," Sage said, pulling Missy close to him the moment she opened the door and led him inside.

She wrapped her arms around his neck. "Hope you're hungry."

"I'm always hungry for you," he said, sticking his tongue down her throat.

As he was kissing and grinding on Missy, his mind traveled back to his encounter with his architect. Sage was perpetually horny and loved sex almost as much as he loved running his family's company. Being at the helm of Hirschfield Publishing afforded him perks that very few were privy to, and he relished every second of being in such an elite group. He knew that if he wasn't CEO of a major corporation, he would have never been allowed inside of Roy Snyderman's private world. Sage wasn't shocked that Roy was a switch-hitter, because he had a distinctive air of class and sophistication, which bordered on homosexuality. Sage thought about calling Roy for some more dick sucking, but he'd broken one of his cardinal rules by mixing business with pleasure, and decided not to deal with Roy personally again until after the studio was complete.

She kissed him back. "Sounds like you want your dessert before dinner."

"I want it now and later," Sage said, running his hands underneath her blouse and rubbing her back.

"Well in that case, let me put the pots on simmer, while we get things heated up in the bedroom," she said, easing out of his embrace and walking into the kitchen. After she turned the fire down on the stove, she walked back over to him, took his hand, and led him into her lair.

Missy wore only an oversized, sheer silk blouse and a bright red thong. Sage could feel his dick rising as he watched her ass sashay underneath the delicate fabric, and he couldn't wait to release his throbbing cock and fuck her good. He began unbuckling his belt and unzipping his pants as they walked down the short hallway, and by the time they reached her bedroom, he had his dick out and was masturbating.

"Come here and let me do that," Missy said, sitting at the foot of the bed.

Sage walked over and waved his semi-erect dick across her face; he then eased the head into her waiting mouth. "I want you to suck me slow and hard, until you taste my cum, and then I want you to start sucking faster and faster and don't stop until I shoot my hot load down your throat," he told her.

Missy couldn't say a word since her tongue was preoccupied, so she just nodded her head and did as instructed.

Sage put his foot on the edge of the bed so that he could feed his dick deeper down her throat. Missy was now sucking his cock fast and furious and the sensation was driving him wild with ecstasy. "That's right, suck that dick, Bitch," he said, grabbing her hair to balance himself as she bobbed up and down on his long rod. Sage felt his semen rising to the top. "Get ready to swallow, Whore, 'cause I'm cumming!" he screamed, holding her hair even tighter. He climaxed with such force that he collapsed onto the bed after he released a mouthful of creamy cum.

"How was dessert?" Missy asked, wiping her mouth with the sleeve of her blouse.

"Hot and sexy, just like I like it," he said, lying on his back with his hands behind his head.

Missy stood up, took off her blouse, and slipped out of her thong. "How about a little reciprocation?" she asked.

Sage turned onto his side, lifted himself by his elbow, and

looked at her crotch. "I thought you were going to get that thing taken care of."

"I plan to. I just need to save a little more money, and then poof, it'll be gone," she said, grabbing her small, flaccid penis.

"Sorry, Babe, you know I don't suck dick, but after the operation, and you have a clit, we can sixty-nine as much as you like," he said, turning over to his stomach and closing his eyes for a catnap.

Missy was born Rico Sanns in Champaign, Illinois, a college town south of Chicago. And though she always felt like a girl inside, she lived her life as a boy until her early twenties. It wasn't until Missy—Rico at the time—graduated college with a degree in dance, and moved to New York, that her life started to change.

Rico met a generous benefactor at a gay club one evening, and he sucked and fucked the old dude so good that the man fell in love and moved Rico into his three-storied town house. The lonely old man was so glad to finally have a full-time lover that he lavished Rico with extravagant gifts and trips abroad; there wasn't anything too good for his boy toy. When Rico expressed his desire to be a woman, his sponsor eagerly agreed to fund the transformation, with the promise that Rico would never leave him for another man. The first step in the long, arduous process was taking female hormones, and after two years his voice was considerably higher, his hair was longer, and his dick was smaller. Next came the saline implants, which gave him a perfect set of 38Ds. With the top half of his body complete, Rico changed his name to Missy, began dressing as a woman full-time, and auditioning for various chorus lines on Broadway. He would tuck his unwanted penis between his legs and wear tight thongs to keep it hidden, and unless he removed the underwear, he looked just like any other woman. But before the final operation to remove his penis and construct a vagina could be performed, his benefactor/lover died of a massive stroke, leaving Missy only half a woman.

From working at Scores and entertaining bi-curious men like Sage—who didn't care that she had a dick, because they preferred to fuck up the ass—she had saved half of the money. Missy thought that it would take her another year to scrape up the rest of the funds for the operation, but fate handed her an unexpected gift. Now it was only a matter of organizing the incriminating evidence that she kept under lock and key, and putting it in the right hands. Missy knew that one day she'd be able to convert the videos and photographs into cash, and fortunately for her, that day was finally here.

18

MASON HAD gone uptown to meet with Trey at the Black Door to talk to him about adding a Poet Sanctuary at the downtown location, where members could recite poems. Only this poetry would have a distinctive edge, almost like the "Vagina Monologues." Mason's vision was for the members to describe their kinkiest sexual experiences in a limerick, while a jazz trio played softly in the background. Trey loved the idea, and before Mason left, they had fleshed out the entire layout. The new chamber would have a round, rotating stage in the middle of the room, and coliseum-style seating, so that no views were obstructed. The room would also have surround-sound speakers throughout, so that the titillating words would reverberate off the walls. Basically, the space would resemble a concert hall, only on a much smaller scale. The meeting had gone extremely well, and Mason was glad that Trey was on-board with his idea. Some bosses could be territorial about their businesses, and only made changes when the initial idea was theirs, but Trey wasn't like that. He embraced new concepts and made Mason feel like part owner instead of just an employee. When Mason left the meeting, he was on cloud nine, and didn't think his night could get any better, but the best was yet to come.

Whoever said that timing was everything could not have coined a more accurate statement in this case. As soon as Mason's taxi pulled up in front of BD2, he spotted Terra taking off a mask outside of the club. Had the taxi arrived a few minutes sooner, she would have seen him coming into the club, and aside from telling her he was a server—which would have dispelled his real estate lie—there was no other way to explain his presence since the Black Door was exclusively for women. And if he'd arrived a few minutes later, he would have missed her altogether. Yes, timing was everything.

He sat there for a few seconds and watched as she walked down the street. Mason was shocked. The last person he expected to see coming out of the Black Door was Ms. Terra Benson. Even though the club's membership list included some of the city's most influential women, she didn't seem like the type who would enjoy the activities that the club offered. She was so proper and refined on the outside, but then again, she did 69 him like a pro at his apartment. Obviously she had a dual personality, and he was intrigued now more than ever to get to know her better.

Once she was a quarter of the way down the block, he got out of the cab and followed her. He didn't know where she was going, nor did he care. All he cared about was finally getting the chance to spend more time with her. He watched her go into Hotel Gansevoort and waited outside a few minutes before going in, so it wouldn't look as if he had been stalking her.

Mason stood on the fringes of the lobby bar and watched Terra settle in and order a drink. He waited until she was sipping comfortably and walked back out to the reservation desk.

"Hi, do you have any suites available tonight?" he asked the reservation clerk.

She typed the date into her computer system, read the screen, and then said, "I'm sorry, sir, all of our suites are booked this evening, but I do have a grand deluxe room available with a city view and a step-out balcony."

"That sounds great. I'll take it," he told her. Mason was hoping that he and Terra would end the evening in each other's arms. He knew it was a stretch. He hadn't seen her since that night in his apartment, but he was desperate and was willing to try just about anything to make love to her again. He gave the clerk his credit card, signed for the room, and returned to the bar area.

Terra was sitting with her back to the door and didn't see him when he came into the lounge. "We've got to stop meeting like this." He smiled as he approached her.

She looked up and was surprised to see Mason. Though she had vowed that their one-night stand was a onetime deal, she was glad to see his face nonetheless. With his cocoa brown skin, smooth bald head, sable eyes, and full lips, he was pleasing to the eyes. He had a face and tall muscular body that resembled Richard T. Jones, the handsome actor from *Judging Amy*. "Are you stalking me?" She smiled back.

If you only knew, he thought. "I was going to ask you the same thing. It seems as if we have the same tastes in lounges," he said, looking at the empty seat next to her.

Terra noticed him staring at the vacant seat. Her mind was telling her not to invite him to sit down, but her heart was saying, *Girl, don't let that man get away.* Terra's mind was racing double time, weighing the pros and cons of having a drink with Mason. On the negative side, if she let him buy her a drink, he would probably think that that was an invitation for a repeat performance of their last tango, but their last tango was HOT, so a repeat performance was also a plus. Terra was still horny from the Black Door, and thought that a little innocent flirtation would take the edge off. "Would you care to sit down?" she said, giving in to the pros.

"I'd love to," he said, and motioned the waitress over. "Can we have a bottle of Veuve Clicquot Grand Dame, please?"

Once the waitress was gone, Terra's tone changed. "You and your bottle service. That's what got me in trouble last time," she said curtly, thinking that he was trying to get her tipsy again.

Mason smiled slyly. "What trouble?"

She looked at him skeptically. "Didn't you see 'Page Six'?"

"Oh, you mean the picture of us coming out of Pravda," he said lightheartedly, as if he hadn't suffered any repercussions from that picture.

"That's the one. Well, just so you know, I plan to walk out of here sober and solo, and not end up in your apartment or in the newspaper," she said, looking him dead in the eyes.

Mason threw his palms in the air, as if surrendering. "Okay, Ms. Benson, whatever you say."

Terra had totally forgotten that the paper mentioned her full name and family legacy. Now he knew that she wasn't just a typical broke wannabe actress; she was a wannabe actress with considerable assets. Her first thought was that he was after her for the money, but then she realized that he'd pursued her before he knew she was Terra Benson, so his interest in her was genuine, and that made her relax a little and get off of the defensive. "I'm sorry. I didn't mean to be so harsh. It's just that I don't want you to get the wrong impression. Contrary to my actions, I'm not into one-night stands, even though I did enjoy myself." She quickly averted her eyes to the floor, as if she were embarrassed, and then looked back into his eyes. "But I can't afford to get drunk and fall into bed with strangers. If it's all right with you, I'd like to erase the past and start fresh."

Starting fresh was more than all right with Mason, because he wanted to forget the morning after, when she disappeared on him. "Sounds good to me. And just so you know, I didn't think you were the one-night stand type of girl anyway. You're much too classy for that," he said, and then thought, *And what's a classy woman like you doing at the Black Door?* He wanted to ask her that question straight out, but didn't want to tip his hand, since he wasn't supposed to know she'd been there in the first place.

"Well, I wouldn't say all that." She blushed.

The waitress brought over the champagne, popped the cork, poured them each a glass, placed the bottle in an ice-filled champagne bucket, put it in the middle of the table, and then left.

"So, are you flying solo tonight? Where's your friend . . . what was her name?" He paused for a second trying to think.

"Lexington, but everyone calls her Lexi. Actually, we were together earlier, but . . ." Terra stopped midsentence, and contemplated whether or not to tell Mason about the Black Door. Well, it wasn't like they were complete strangers; he had eaten her out in the backseat of a taxi. ". . . we decided to go our separate ways," she said, finishing her sentence. "You won't believe where we were earlier," she said, almost in a whisper, deciding to tell him after all.

"Where?" he asked, even though he knew what she was about to say.

"This club called the Black Door."

"Is it a dance club?" he asked, feigning ignorance.

"Not exactly," she said, with the corners of her mouth turning up into a slight smile. She moved a little closer to him and whispered, "It's an erotic club exclusively for women."

He put his index finger and thumb to his chin and rubbed his goatee. "Really? Tell me more."

"Well, I don't know a lot about the club because it's for members only and I'm not a member. Tonight was my first time there."

"How did you get in if it's for members only?" He wanted to know. Now he was more than curious, because there was no way she should have been allowed to enter if she wasn't a member.

"Lexi's a member, and she borrowed her friend's mask and password so that I could check out the club."

Mason made a mental note to revamp the entrance security, since clearly there was a loophole with the current system. "So, what did you think about the club?"

"It was hot, actually a little too hot for me. I guess I'm more of a private person, and making love with a bunch of strangers watching isn't my thing." No sooner had Terra made the statement than she thought back to Mason eating her out in the taxi, and how she got off on the driver hearing them. She felt like a hypocrite, and didn't know how to clarify that comment, so she picked up her flute and took a huge gulp.

"So . . . you're not into PDAs," he said, looking at her like he couldn't believe what she had just said.

"Okay, you got me. Public displays of affection are fine, especially in the backseat of a taxi," she mused.

He also thought back to that erotic cab ride and said, "Yes, they are."

She finished her champagne and put the flute down. "Look, Mason, it was great running into you tonight, but I'm not going down that road again. What happened between us was a onetime thing, and it can't happen anymore. I've got too much on my plate to get involved with you," she said point-blank, and got up to leave.

"Wait a minute." He reached out for her hand. "Can't I at least have your cell number, so we can go out for coffee sometime?" he asked.

Terra thought about it for a split second, but remembered her stalled seduction plan, and that she needed to concentrate on winning Sage over, instead of focusing on Mason. "No, I don't think that'll be a good idea. Let's leave things the way they are. Take care of yourself," she said, and walked out before he had a chance to plead his case.

Mason was shocked, for the second time that evening. He hadn't seen that coming. A few minutes ago they were talking and drinking champagne, and he thought for sure that he'd have the opportunity to win her over, but she shot down his hopes like a clay pigeon. He poured more champagne into his flute, and proceeded to drown his sorrows. Mason polished off the first bottle and ordered a second one. As he was sipping his bubbly and licking his wounds, he heard a voice from behind.

"You won't believe it, but there are at least twenty photographers outside."

He turned around, and there was Terra looking panicky.

"I was getting ready to leave, and before I could step a foot outside, one of them saw me through the glass door, and they all started calling my name. I don't know how they knew I was here," she said, pacing back and forth.

"Calm down. It's going to be all right," he said, touching the side of her arm. "Why don't you sit down and have another glass of Veuve, while we figure out what to do?" Mason was totally elated that she was trapped. He didn't particularly care for the paparazzi because they were always sticking their lenses where they didn't belong, but at the moment he was loving them, since they were the reason Terra was back and acting like a damsel in distress.

"I know I shouldn't be freaked out, but I don't want my picture in the paper again. Once they get a taste of someone's private life, it's like their need to pry is insatiable, and they keep coming back for more and more until your every move is documented. Frankly, I don't want to live underneath a microscope, with the whole world in my business. My personal life is just that—personal!" she fumed.

Mason could see that she was getting madder by the second, and he needed to calm her down quickly, before she stormed out and gave the photographers a piece of her mind. "I might have the perfect solution," he said, getting her attention.

"What? Anything you can think of would be greatly appreciated," she said, sounding desperate.

"I have a room upstairs. A friend of mine manages the hotel and gives me a great deal anytime I want to stay downtown. And since I've been drinking tonight, I didn't feel like fighting the masses for a taxi back uptown," he lied. He certainly wasn't going to admit that he'd booked the room in the hopes of fucking her all night.

At first Terra looked at him with disbelief, but she was between a brick and a boulder. She could take her chances with the paparazzi, and wind up in every tabloid from here to Iceland, or she could go with Mason and spare herself another embarrassing close up. "Okay, I'll go upstairs with you, but only until they leave and then I can go home in peace," she said, laying down her terms.

"No problem. I'll even come back downstairs in about an hour to make sure that they're gone," he said, sweetening the deal. Mason motioned the waitress back over and told her to send the remainder of the champagne upstairs.

Terra was still fidgety once they were inside the room. "They must have been following me," she said, looking out the window trying to see down to the sidewalk, but their view was facing east and the entrance to the hotel was west. "I pray that no photographers were lurking around when I left the Black Door. That's the last thing I need," she said, nearly on the verge of tears.

"Don't worry about that, because I'm sure if they had snapped your picture coming out of an erotica club, then no one would have followed you here. If you think about it, a picture in front of a club like the Black Door is much more valuable than a picture of you coming out of a hotel alone," he said, trying to ease her nerves.

Terra hadn't thought about the situation from that angle. "Actually, that makes perfect sense," she said, finally feeling a sense of relief.

After the bellhop brought the champagne to the room, Mason and Terra settled on the sofa and began chatting to pass the time.

"So how's the real estate business?" she asked.

"It can be hectic at times, but I do enjoy sealing the deal," he said, smiling. "And how's the acting thing going?"

"Well, I haven't heard from my agent all week. I guess she's pissed at me for blowing my last audition."

"What was the audition for?" he asked. He could care less about the audition, but wanted to keep her talking so that she wouldn't leave anytime soon.

"It was for a new Dove soap product. The lines were simple, but I got nervous and flubbed them."

"Better luck next time." He smiled.

An hour quickly swept by, and Terra said, "Do you think they're still outside?"

"No, but I'll go downstairs to make sure."

Mason took the elevator down and checked the front of the hotel. There were no photographers in sight, and the bar was practically empty. When he got back to the room, she was standing at the window.

"Well, what's the verdict?" she asked.

"They're still camped outside, and I even saw two photographers posing as customers inside of the lobby," he told her.

Terra fell into his arms, sobbing. "Oh, God, why can't they just leave me alone and follow someone else?"

Mason held her close and stroked the back of her hair. "Don't cry. Everything's going to be okay." He suddenly felt bad for lying, but not bad enough to tell her the truth. He knew that if he did, she'd be out of there faster than a hummingbird in motion. Instead, he rocked her back and forth.

Terra held on to him like he was her savior. She felt safe in his arms, like nothing could hurt her as long as his strong arms were wrapped around her.

Mason felt her trembling and held her tighter. They stood like that for what seemed like hours, but it had only been a couple of minutes. Mason leaned down and kissed the top of her head. He wanted so badly to protect her from everything bad, even though he had manipulated the situation to his advantage. When she didn't shy away from that benign kiss, he kissed her forehead, and when she still didn't shy away, he leaned down closer and gently kissed her lips.

Terra didn't want to respond to him, but the chemistry between them was too powerful, and she couldn't resist, so she gave in and kissed him back.

Without taking his lips from hers, he slowly guided her toward the king-sized bed and sat her down on the comforter, all the while kissing her passionately. He stopped momentarily to remove her shoes, stockings, and leather skirt, and then resumed kissing.

She untied her halter top, and her titties sprang loose. She lay back naked on the bed and watched and waited for him to take off his clothes. His body was sheer perfection. His pectorals were chiseled, and his abdominals were rippled like an old-fashioned washboard; but the best body part of all was his thick, ten-inch dick, which was erect and as hard as a piston. Terra felt her pussy getting wetter and wetter in anticipation of receiving his long rod.

Mason eased in between her legs and kissed her perky nipples. He then fingered the folded petals of her vagina, found her clit, and began rubbing it with his thumb and index finger.

"Oh . . . Baby . . . yes!" she moaned in between gasps for air.

Hearing her moan in ecstasy was making him hornier, and he couldn't wait any longer, so he eased the head of his penis inside her slippery canal and began slowly pumping in and out. He caressed her face and said, "Look at me."

Terra looked into his eyes and felt a deeper connection with him. She felt like she was falling in love. She tried to fight the feeling by averting her eyes, but the pull was too strong and kept drawing her eyes back to his, and she knew at that very moment that they were not just fucking; they were making love. She wrapped her arms around his neck, pulling him in closer, and slowly moved her hips to match his gentle thrusts. No man had ever made love to her like this—not even Professor Langston—so she closed her eyes and surrendered to the feeling. They made love for hours, until they were both exhausted and fell off to sleep.

Mason began to stir as the bright sun peeked into the window. He was holding on to something soft and cuddly, but was afraid to open his eyes. He couldn't bear the thought of waking up to another pillow. He wanted so badly to be holding Terra, but he knew there was a possibility that she had skipped out like before, leaving him caressing an inanimate object. To lessen the shock of reality, he slowly opened one eye and looked to see what he was holding. There in his arms was Terra, sound asleep. Mason smiled from ear to ear, and watched her dream. He held her a little tighter, because this time there was no way he was letting her get away.

19

TERRA WAS sleeping so soundly that she dreamed she was
in her own comfortable bed with the Egyptian cotton sheets and
fluffy down comforter. She rolled over and opened her eyes to look
at the clock on her nightstand, but the clock didn't look familiar;
neither did the nightstand. Her eyes slowly scanned the room, and
the instant she realized that she wasn't at home, snippets of the
previous night flashed through her mind like a movie trailer playing only the best scenes. Terra remembered her and Mason making
love and the memory made her tingle all over. She looked to her
left and saw what appeared to be a body lying underneath the covers. She flipped back the comforter thinking that he was cuddled
up sleeping, but it was only a heap of pillows. She glanced around
the room, but didn't see him anywhere; the only thing she saw
were clothes strewn across the floor and on the furniture. Her
shoes, stockings, and skirt were at the foot of the bed; his jeans
were on the side of the bed; his shirt was tossed across the arm of a

chair and his shoes were kicked underneath a desk. She surveyed the aftermath, and their clothes told the story of a lustful seduction. She grabbed her halter top that was lying on top of the nightstand and tried to cover herself with it as she made her way to the bathroom.

"Good morning, Sweetheart," Mason said, coming out of the bathroom wearing his boxers. He pulled her to him, engulfing her in a bear hug. "How'd you sleep?"

Standing there in the buff, trying to cover her breasts with the small top, she felt slightly embarrassed. "Like I was at home in my own bed," she said.

"Yeah, I could see that you were comfortable, because when I got up to take a shower, you were snoring lightly," he said, kissing the top of her head.

"Really? I don't normally snore." She blushed.

"It must have been my good loving that knocked you out cold," he teased.

"I guess I should call you Sominex," she teased back, getting over her awkwardness and looking up at him. He was freshly shaved, and not one hair on his goatee was out of place. Her appearance on the other hand was beyond disheveled. "Let me jump in the shower and freshen up," she said, easing out of his embrace and running her hand through her unruly hair trying to smooth it down.

Forty minutes later, Terra reemerged with a white towel wrapped around her hair, and wearing a fuzzy, hotel-monogrammed, terrycloth robe. She had soaked her body in the Jacuzzi tub before washing her hair in the shower. She felt renewed and ready to start her day. The only thing missing was her morning latte.

"Hey, Beautiful, I didn't think you were ever coming out of there. Are you hungry?"

"As a matter of fact, I'm starving," she said, with her stomach suddenly growling. Normally she didn't eat breakfast, but last night with their acrobatic lovemaking, she had woken up with an appetite.

He was sitting at a small, white linen—covered dining table near the window. "Come here."

Terra walked over and saw several plates covered with silver warming domes. She sat down, looked at the exquisitely set table with china plates and crystal glassware, and said, "What have we here?"

"I didn't know what you liked, so I ordered a variety of stuff." He took the lid off the first plate and said, "We have mixed berries, nuts, yogurt, and fresh-squeezed orange juice for a healthy start to the day." He removed the dome off of another plate. "And for a semihealthy start, there are bagels, lox, and chive cream cheese." He uncovered the next to last dish. "Now for the pièce de résistance"—he waved his hand over the meal for a dramatic effect—"pancakes with maple syrup, scrambled eggs, and country smoked bacon. This may not be the healthiest choice, but it sure is the tastiest. So"—he gave her a devilish grin—"what's it going to be, Ms. Benson?"

"Hmm." She looked at each delicious meal. "I'm thinking about this one," she said, pointing to the fattening pancakes and bacon.

"A woman after my own heart, but I would've pegged you for a yogurt and fruit type person."

"On those rare occasions when I do eat breakfast, it is usually fruit and yogurt, but it's not every day that I get to indulge in my favorite breakfast of all time," she said, taking a stack of the fluffy cakes. "I wish I had a latte. Then my morning would be complete," she said, pouring syrup over the short stack.

He took the dome off of the last dish. "Your wish is my command."

Terra looked, and in the middle of the plate was a Borders latte. "Oh, wow!" she exclaimed. "How did you know I'm crazy about the latte at Borders, and when did you go out and get it?"

"You were drinking a latte the day we met, so I called a messenger service and had one delivered especially for you."

"Oh, Mason, that's so sweet, but how'd you know I was drinking a latte, and not a plain cup of coffee?" she asked, curious to know.

"I noticed everything about you that day, from the way the sun highlighted your hair to your perfect posture. I even noticed your Hermès tote," he said, as if it were yesterday. "Besides, I could smell the Chai flavorings."

Terra was flabbergasted. His attention to detail was amazing. Most men didn't know the difference between Hermès or H&M, nor could they distinguish Chai from cinnamon. She was loving this man more and more by the second. First, he saved her from the paparazzi, and then made exquisite love to her all night. Now he was making love to her taste buds. She felt like a pampered princess as she sat back and enjoyed her royal breakfast.

"If you're not busy today, I thought we'd walk over to SoHo and check out a few galleries, and then have a late lunch," he said hopefully.

Terra couldn't remember the last time she had bopped in and out of the art galleries in SoHo, and loved the idea of discovering new artists and spending the afternoon with her new love. "I would like that very much."

"Great. How about we leave in about fifteen minutes?" he said, polishing off the last piece of bacon.

"Sounds good," she said, standing up to get dressed, but then she remembered the black leather miniskirt, matching halter, and red, four-inch sandals that she had worn last night. The outfit was perfect for partying, but not for gallery hopping. "I'm going to need more than fifteen minutes."

"Why? What's wrong?" he asked, hoping she hadn't changed her mind.

"My outfit," she said, picking the black leather skirt up off the floor.

"What's the matter with it?" he asked, seeing nothing wrong.

"Nothing if I want to look like a rocker in the middle of the day, which is not my style." She walked over to her purse, which was sitting on the sofa, reached in and took out her cell phone. "I'm going to call my personal shopper at Bergdorf and have her pick out something more appropriate," she told him, and hit the speed dial to the store. "Terra Benson calling for Anne Thomas," she said, changing her tone to a more businesslike one. "Hi, Anne. Yes, I'm fine, thank you. Anne, I need for you to pull together a pair of Seven jeans with the antique denim finish, a baby-doll top, one of those cute short blazers, a pair of comfortable Tod's for walking, and a pair of oversized Gucci shades. And I'll need all of that messengered over to Hotel Gansevoort as soon as humanly possible." She covered the mouthpiece with her hand, and asked Mason their room number. Once he gave her that information, she returned to the call. "Oh, and I'll also need a Tod's tote to match the shoes. Great! Thanks, Anne," she said, and flipped her phone shut.

Mason was speechless. It was easy to forget that she was an heiress, because she was so down-to-earth with him, but hearing her spend what must have been close to three thousand dollars, in less than sixty seconds and all without even giving a credit card number or her sizes, brought home the reality that she was mega-rich.

An hour and a half later the bellhop was knocking on the door with lavender shopping bags from Bergdorf Goodman. Mason tipped him, and handed over the merchandise to Terra, who went into the bathroom and made a quick change from the bathrobe into street clothes.

Mason whistled the second she stepped out of the bathroom. She was beautiful in the robe, but dressed in the trendy outfit with her hair loose in soft curls, she looked like a fashion model. "Not bad." He whistled again. "You're going to have to give that personal shopper a personal thank you from me."

Terra blushed, and stuffed her clothes from the night before in the tote, put on her shades, and headed toward the door, but she hesitated, suddenly remembering the reason why she had spent the night in the first place. "You don't think the paparazzi are still lurking outside do you?"

Mason knew that the photographers were long gone, since they had packed up their cameras last night (unbeknown to Terra). "Don't worry, I'm more than sure that they're somewhere else, stalking another victim. Come on, Sweetheart, I'll protect you," he said, putting his arm around her shoulders.

As they left the hotel arm in arm, they were totally unaware that someone was lurking in the shadows, snapping pictures of their every move.

20

IT HAD been forty-eight hours, but Mason was still flying high from his marathon date with Terra. After leaving the hotel, they strolled arm and arm over to SoHo, and moseyed in and out of some of the most expensive galleries in Manhattan. Nothing really caught their eye, until they walked over to West Broadway, where some of the best painters and sculptors in the city sold their work on the sidewalk. As they admired the talent of the street artists, Terra fell in love with a five-foot still life painting of a half empty bottle of imported vodka and two martini glasses garnished with plumb green olives, sitting atop a long wooden bar. She said that the painting reminded her of the night at Pravda where they laughed and drank themselves silly. Watching how much she admired the piece, Mason immediately bought it for her so that she could always remember their first night together. So they wouldn't have to lug the huge canvas around town, the artist agreed to have the painting delivered to her apartment the following day.

During lunch, they shared a bottle of pinot grigio and a large bowl of farfalle with smoked salmon and asparagus at Barolo's outdoor garden. Mason felt as if they were on holiday in Tuscany, instead of in New York. Though neither broached the subject of dating exclusively, their actions spoke volumes. The way she leaned her head on his shoulder as they walked down the street, and the way he fed her forks full of pasta, it was like they were already in a committed relationship. They were so comfortable together it was as if they'd known each other for years. After a leisurely lunch, they parted ways, with Terra thanking him for a lovely afternoon, and Mason promising to call her the next day, and then they each got in separate taxis. Terra went home, and Mason went to the club.

THOUGH THAT WAS two days ago, Mason couldn't get the thought of her out of his mind. Even the scantily clad members at the club couldn't distract him. Normally, he wouldn't have been able to exert any self-control as he walked through the club in search of a pair of ripe titties to suck on and a wet pussy to fuck. But tonight, he was all business as he went from chamber to chamber trying to decide which room to convert into the Poet Sanctuary.

Mason walked past the window that looked into the Voyeurism Room and saw something that caught his eye and made him stop in his tracks. There, in the middle of the king-sized bed, was a woman lying on her back, buck naked, wearing a multicolored mask with long pink, yellow, teal, red, and tangerine plumes. Her nipples were being sucked by one server, which wasn't strange at all, but what made Mason stop and stare was the dick between her legs that another server was sucking. From where he stood, he couldn't see if she was a hermaphrodite or a transgender who hadn't got the bottom half done yet. Mason had never seen a chick with a dick before——at least not in person——and watching her receive pleasure on both ends was fascinating. He stood there until the server made her climax and a stream of cum squirted out of her tiny penis. But that wasn't the end of the show. After she came, she got on all fours and knelt down on her elbows so that her ass was high in the air, turned around and told the servers to fuck her. The one who had been sucking her tits watched and waited as the other server stuck his tool up her ass and went to work. He was humping so hard that sweat poured off of his body onto hers. After a few minutes, he pulled out, so that the other server could pull up to the bumper. Mason watched them tag team her, and then in a sudden turn of events, they each stroked their own dicks and came simultaneously.

Damn, now that's some freaky shit, Mason thought, and once the show was over, he continued on his way.

Mason stood in the doorway of the Disco, which was pumping with pulsating bodies dancing the night away, and knew that was one room that wouldn't be replaced. He then continued down the corridor and peeked his head into the Naked Pool room, which was full of members playing Eight Ball in the buff. Naked pool was so popular that Mason knew this room was also here to stay. As he surveyed the Aphrodisiac Bistro and the Chocolate Chamber, which were both buzzing with members and servers, Mason realized that he couldn't justifiably get rid of those theme rooms either. The only alternative to eliminating one of the existing rooms was to expand upstairs where his office was located. There were a couple of empty storage spaces that could be converted into the Poet Sanctuary.

As he turned around and walked back down the hallway, a member with an elaborate mask approached him.

"Hey there, where's the fire?" she asked, rubbing her hand up and down his chest.

"What do you mean?" he said, taking a slight step away from her.

"You're rushing off like there's a four-alarm fire somewhere," she said, taking a step closer.

Mason took one look at her mask with the multicolored feathers and realized that "she was the he" or was "he the she"? In any case, it was the same chick with the dick who had just gotten fucked by two servers. He immediately looked down at her crotch, thinking that he would see a bulge, but he didn't. She wore a tight, hot pink thong, and was as smooth as a board. *Must be holding her little dick in place.* He couldn't help but stare at her beautiful 38Ds. They were perfectly round with nipples at least three-quarters of an inch long that poked through the sheer blouse she wore.

"You wanna suck 'em?" she asked, noticing him looking.

"No," he quickly said, returning his gaze to her masked face.

She unbuttoned her blouse and began tweaking her nipples until they grew harder. She then put her hands underneath each titty and started bouncing them up and down. "They look good enough to eat, don't they?"

Mason was a breast man, and had to admit that her boobs were big and juicy, just the way he liked them. He was tempted to take a taste test, but was stopped by the thought of Terra, his true love. Even though she would never know whether or not he fucked around, he would know, and he didn't want to live with the guilt. "Yeah, they do, but I'm going to have to take a pass."

"Since when does Mason Anthony take a pass when he could be sucking and fucking?" she asked.

How the hell does she know my name? he thought frantically. Mason always wore his mask when he perused the club, so there was no way she could have seen his face. "What did you say?" Even though he had heard her, he wanted to make sure she hadn't mistaken him for someone else.

She grabbed his hand and put it on her titty. "Doesn't that feel good, Mason?"

He snatched his hand away. "Who are you?"

She reached in back of her head and untied her mask. "Don't you recognize me?"

Mason searched her full lips, high cheekbones, and hazel eyes, but he couldn't place her face. "No, I don't."

"It's me, Rico," she said.

He squinted his eyes and looked at her hard. "Rico?"

Mason had met Rico Sanns in college. He had been at Champaign, Urbana, on a four-year football scholarship, studying premed, and Rico had been a dance major. At the coach's suggestion, the varsity team took a semester of dance to help with their dexterity. While Mason was the star on the field, Rico was the star on the floor. He was a graceful dancer and could perform the most difficult moves with ease. Most of the other dance majors found the presence of the clumsy football players intrusive and resented them taking up space in their domain. But not Rico. He welcomed the beefy athletes and did whatever he could to help them with their dance routines. Mason stood out from the crowd, not because he was the cutest player, but because he was the clumsiest, and Rico immediately gravitated toward him.

Mason had taken one look at Rico prancing around in his super-tight leotards and belly shirt and knew that he was gay. Mason had a gay uncle, so he was familiar with the mannerisms of an overtly feminine man. Having grown up around the rainbow coalition, Mason didn't take offense when Rico tried to befriend him, but he made it clear that he was straight and had recently started dating Heather Scott, captain of the debate team. As it turned out, Rico and Heather had known each other since freshman year and were quite close, so the three of them often hung out together. Most weekends, Rico could be found camped out on the couch in Heather's off-campus apartment.

One Saturday evening, while Heather was at her sorority house for a meeting, Mason and Rico were at the apartment drinking beer and watching basketball. After polishing off nearly a case of MGD, they both passed out drunk on the sofa, and when Mason came to, Rico was between his legs sucking his dick. At first, Mason thought that it was Heather, but when his eyes finally focused, he realized that it was Rico. Mason wanted to tell him to stop, but Rico was sucking his dick and licking his balls like no woman had before and the sensation felt beyond good; it was like a natural high. The liquor flowing through his veins clouded his reasoning. He wanted to get up, but his body wouldn't move, so he closed his eyes and pretended like Heather was giving him head instead of Rico.

Over the course of the semester, from time to time, Rico would beg Mason to let him suck him off, and against his better judgment, Mason agreed, because he wanted that supernatural feeling again. They would meet at Heather's apartment when she was in class, and Rico would do all the work, while Mason laid back and got his helmet buffed.

Feeling guilty about letting another man suck his dick, and cheating on his girlfriend, Mason finally ended the one-sided affair. That was Mason's first and last time experiencing oral sex with a man, and once he graduated, he left the memory of his sordid sexual act behind him on the college campus, and never thought about Rico again.

"Yeah, it's me," Missy said, dropping her high-pitched voice and sounding more like a man.

Mason was so full of questions that he didn't know where to begin. "How . . . uh . . . where . . ." he stammered. "How did you know it was me behind this mask?" he finally asked.

"Initially, I didn't know, but after I sucked your dick in the Aphrodisiac Bistro, I started putting two and two together."

Mason looked totally confused. "What?"

"Remember that night in the bistro, when my friend Princess— she had on a pewter and gold mask with black feathers—and I took you to one of the booths in the back? I sucked your dick, while you sucked her titties?"

As she described the encounter, Mason began to get a visual of that night and silently cursed himself for fucking around with the members, but it was too late for brow beating. He reluctantly nodded his head yes.

"Well, I thought I knew that dick, but I wasn't completely sure, so later that night, instead of going home, I waited for you to come out of the club. You didn't have on your mask, but I knew you were the same guy that I had just sucked off, because I recognized your tight jeans and wife-beater. Anyway, I followed you home, and when I saw your picture on 'Page Six,' I started thinking about old times and wanted to reconnect," Missy said, her voice now back in the higher register.

"When I got your note, I was wondering how you knew where I lived," Mason mumbled more to himself than to her.

"I've been waiting for your call, so that we could pick up where we left off, but then it occurred to me that you were not coming to me, so I had to come to you. Besides, I have another more important matter to talk to you about," she said, taking a step closer to him.

"Look, Rico, or whatever your name is now——"

She cut him off. "It's Missy. My new name is Missy."

"Whatever. Look, we're not picking up anywhere, and I don't care what you have to say. What happened in college is ancient history, and I have no plans of revisiting the past," he said sternly, and started to walk away.

Missy grabbed Mason's arm. "Wait a minute. You're not going to dismiss me like you did in college. Before you walk away, you should know that I have a few mementos from back in the day that the tabloids would love to get their hands on."

"And why would the tabloids care about information on me? I'm not famous."

"I know you're not famous. That's why I've held on to this stuff for so long, because up until now it was meaningless, but now that you're dating a celebrity it's finally come in handy." Missy smirked as she watched Mason's expression slowly turn to one of horror. "I'm sure that the tabloids would be interested to know that Terra Benson's 'buffed beau,'" she said, using the term from "Page Six," "likes to get his helmet 'buffed' by the boys."

"There's no way you can link me with Terra," he said, panicked. "That picture in *The Post* didn't even have my name in the caption."

"Oh, I can link you all right," Missy said, taking out a set of digital pictures from her purse and showing them to him.

Mason snatched the pictures out of her hand and stared in disbelief. He and Terra's entire day in SoHo had been documented, from the moment they stepped out of the hotel, to their romp on West Broadway, and even their cozy lunch. And unlike the picture in the paper, which only showed them coming out of a lounge, these pictures clearly showed that they were an item. He ripped the photographs to shreds and threw the pieces at Missy. "That's what I think of your pictures."

"Not to worry, I have several sets, as well as video footage of me sucking your dick." Unbeknown to Mason, Rico had set up a camcorder in Heather's apartment and recorded their head games. It was Rico's practice to videotape most of his sexual encounters and sell them to the freakiest bidder. He used the money from the X-rated tapes to subsidize his tuition. Fortunately, he had held on to the tape of Mason, because that was his favorite and he kept it in his private collection.

Missy continued. "Now if it was anyone else besides Terra Benson, the tobacco heiress, all of this would be irrelevant. But you know how hungry the press is to bite into her personal life. That's why I called the tabloids the moment I saw you go into Hotel Gansevoort. I had a feeling that Terra was inside. You managed to dodge them, but you couldn't hide from my trusty camera"— Missy smiled snidely—"and I think they would just eat this information up, don't you?"

The panic returned, rendering Mason speechless. He had finally found the woman of his dreams. Now that dream was being threatened by an ugly nightmare. "I have money. Just tell me how much you want," he said, wanting all of this to go away.

"I don't want your money. I want Terra's. She must be worth a few billion, and all I'm asking for is a measly million," Missy said in a deadpan tone, and then turned the corners of her mouth up into a sly *Cat in the Hat*-type grin.

"You must be crazy!" Mason shouted. "How am I supposed to get my hands on her money?"

"I don't care how you do it, just do it. You have until next week, and if I don't have a certified check in my hands for one million dollars, then the pictures, as well as the videos, will be all over the news," Missy said, and strutted away.

Mason wanted to run after Rico, throw him down, and wring his scrawny neck, but a murder rap was far worse than incriminating pictures. He needed to come up with a plan, and soon, because if he wanted to keep Terra, he had to protect her from this crazy blackmail scheme.

21

"HOW CUTE is this?" Terra asked, holding up a short cashmere midriff sweater. She and Lexi were shopping at the Prada boutique on Fifth Avenue.

Lexi lightly fingered the soft material. "It's all right," she said, barely giving the sweater any attention. Earlier, Lexi had asked Terra what she did after she left the Black Door, and Terra had been extremely vague. Now Lexi was irritated because she knew that her friend was hiding something and she wanted to know what it was. "Put that sweater down and tell me what happened the other night," she demanded.

Terra hadn't told Lexi about her rendezvous with Mason because that night and the next day had been a magical time for the two of them, and she wasn't ready to share their private moments for fear that talking about it would ruin the spell. Seeing the sour look on Lexi's face, she realized that if she didn't give her friend blow-by-blow details, their friendship might be ruined instead.

Terra glanced over her shoulder making sure that no one was within earshot, and then told Lexi exactly what happened that night. "Girl, the next day was so perfect that we hated to leave each other. It felt like we were in one of those corny romance movies, where the two lovers can't stand being apart," she said, her eyes glazing over with a dreamy look.

After hearing the entire story and seeing the look of love on Terra's face, Lexi was sorry she'd asked. It didn't take a rocket scientist to see that Terra was in love. Thinking that she should have been with Mason instead of her friend, a twinge of jealousy shot through Lexi. He was her type of man, and besides, she had seen him first that night at Pravda. But Terra had won by default since she'd bumped into him at the coffee shop. In any event, it didn't matter, because they were in love. "So"—she gave Terra an all-knowing look—"it sounds like you're in love with this guy."

Terra blushed and her cheeks turned candy-apple red. "Is it that obvious?"

"Yep, it's all over your face, but are you sure you're not taking this too fast?" Lexi asked in a slightly discouraging way.

"I realize we just met a few weeks ago, but I feel so comfortable with him. It's like we've known each other for years. Usually I'm more reserved, but there's something about Mason that makes me want to be a wild woman. He's broken down all of my inhibitions, and—"

"I thought Professor Langston did that," Lexi sniped.

"David taught me how to fuck, but Mason has taught me how to make love, and there's such a distinct difference," Terra replied with that dreamy-eyed look again.

Lexi had never been in love, so she couldn't understand exactly what Terra was saying. "What's the difference?"

"When you're deeply in love with someone and he feels the same way, sex is not just an act, but an extension of the love you feel for each other. And every time you make love, your feelings are magnified a hundred times."

Listening to Terra's words, Lexi knew that she had never really made love. "You make it sound so romantic."

"It is. Just wait until you fall in love and then you'll know what I truly mean."

Hearing her friend sound so elated, Lexi couldn't help but feel happy for Terra even though a tiny part of her still felt envious. "Well, when I meet Mr. Right, I'm sure the sparks will fly just like with you and Mason. So, now that you've found Prince Charming, what are you going to do about Sage?" she asked, changing the subject.

In her current state of bliss, Terra had forgotten about hatching another plan to star in Sage's first production. "Trying to seduce him is completely out of the question now that I'm involved with Mason. And it's not like that plan was working anyway. Maybe I'll take your suggestion and have my agent set me up with a screen test."

"If you get the part, just remember to give me my twenty percent consultation fee." Lexi laughed, returning to her old self.

"Twenty percent? You're too damn expensive! I think I'm going to have to find another consultant." She laughed too. Then Terra's phone rang.

"Hello?" she said, once she fished the gadget out of her purse.

"Hey, sweetheart, it's me," said Mason.

"Hey, yourself." She smiled into the tiny phone.

"Where are you?" he asked in a hushed tone.

"At Prada on Fifth Avenue with Lexi. What's going on? Why are you whispering? I can barely hear you."

"I'm not whispering," he said, raising his voice a decibel, trying to sound normal. "Are you busy tonight?"

"Busy seeing you," she teased.

"Can you meet me at my apartment around nine o'clock?" he asked, dropping his voice again, as if someone might be listening.

"Sounds like a clandestine rendezvous," she said, picking up on his lower register.

"You remember where I live, don't you?" he asked, ignoring her comment.

"Yes. I'll see you at nine!" she said excitedly.

"Okay, see you then," he said, and hung up.

She walked over to Lexi, who was looking through a rack of black dresses. "That was 'my man.'" She beamed. "He wants me to come over tonight."

"I see you're claiming him already," Lexi commented, her jealousy returning.

"Yep, I sure am," she said, clueless as to her friend's true feelings. Terra held up a skimpy black dress with leather spaghetti straps. "This is perfect for tonight." She bounced to the register and gave the saleswoman her black AmEx, without paying any attention to the fifteen-hundred-dollar price tag.

Lexi followed close behind, and bought a similar dress and matching shoes. Once outside, the women hopped into Terra's waiting Maybach, and headed downtown to Helmut Lang's flagship boutique. They were like kids in toyland inside the gallerylike space, and the hours flew by as they tried on piece after fabulously designed piece. With armloads of skirts, pants, blouses, and jackets, they handed over their plastic with ease, paid for their treasures, and returned to the car.

"Once I drop you off, I'm going to take a nice, long, hot bath, put on my new dress, and go see my new man!" Terra gushed.

"Ask Mason if he has any available friends," Lexi said, realizing that jealousy would do nothing but burn a hole in her stomach, so she decided to join the "lovers' club," and find a man of her own.

"I'll ask him. I hope he does, and then we can double date.

Wouldn't that be fun?" Terra was so happy that she nearly sang her words.

"Yeah, it would be. Call me tomorrow and let me know what he said. If he doesn't have any available friends, I think I'll join one of those online dating services, because I'm not meeting any mature men out at the bars. They all seem to be young and silly."

"I thought you liked them like that."

"I thought I did too, but they don't have any couth. All they want to do is fuck, which is fine for the first week or two, but then I want some substance. After hearing about your gallery-hopping lunch date, it made me realize that I need a more mature man," she confessed.

"Don't worry, Lexi." Terra patted her friend's leg. "We'll find you a good man, like Mason."

"Thanks, Girl."

Terra dropped Lexi off at her apartment, and told Leroy to wait out front once he pulled up to her building. She went upstairs, spread her new outfit on the bed, and took a long soak in her spa-type tub. After her rejuvenating bath, she smoothed Molton Brown's rich emollient all over her skin. Terra had a tiny waist, slender hips, and a cute bump of a butt. Unlike the rest of her diminutive body parts, her breasts were large and looked fake, but were supple, unlike false boobs. She loved her 36Cs, even though she rarely showed them off. Usually she hid her voluptuous rack underneath support bras and loose shirts, because she didn't want to cause any unwanted attention. But not tonight. Tonight, she wanted all of Mason's attention.

She walked out of the adjoining bathroom, into her bedroom, and slipped into her new Prada dress. The sensuous jersey fabric clung to her body and showcased her favorite asset. Terra stepped over to the mirror and admired how inviting her nipples looked through the thin material. She turned to the side and checked out the profile of her tiny tush. She patted her tight butt and felt extremely sexy, since she didn't have on a stitch of underwear, not even a thong. And to cap off the sexy number, she slid her feet into a pair of rhinestone Choos.

Terra walked back into the bathroom and fluffed out the curls in her hair. She dusted her face with a light translucent power, applied a layer of cherry-scented gloss to her lips, and sprayed her neck, cleavage, and wrists with her signature perfume. She opened the medicine cabinet, took out a travel toothbrush (for in the morning), and put it in her evening bag. She took one last look in the mirror before heading downstairs to her waiting car.

Mason's apartment was just a few blocks away, and she could have walked but wanted to arrive in style. Besides, she didn't have on walking shoes. She introduced herself to his doorman, and waited while he called up and announced her arrival.

"Damn, Baby." Mason stood back and took in her new look. She looked completely different from the other day, when she had worn jeans and a blazer. "You look scrumptious." He hadn't expected Terra to show up looking like she just stepped off the pages of *Black Tail*. He'd invited her over to talk, so that he could get a feel of whether or not he could tell her the truth about his past. He was in love with Terra and didn't want any secrets between them. Secrets were like dormant cancer cells, waiting to strike when your defenses were down. He was experiencing a serious bout of detrimental secrets and wanted to stop the cancer before it spread, but watching her stand there with her nipples poking through the dress, all he could think about was making love to her.

She turned around so that he could get the full view. "You like what you see?"

"Like?" He pulled her to him. "I love!"

Terra wrapped her arms around his neck and pressed her titties into his chest. "Good. I bought this dress just for you."

He leaned down and put his lips dangerously close to hers, so close that he could smell the fruity scent of her lip gloss. "You wore this for me?" he asked, nearly touching her lips with his.

"I sure did," she said softly.

Mason moved his lips to her neck and took a deep whiff. "Did you wear this intoxicating perfume for me too?"

"Uh hum," she moaned, unable to get out a proper sentence because he was mesmerizing her with his subtle seduction.

Mason pressed his groin into her crotch. "What else did you wear for me?" He rubbed her ass through the dress and didn't feel any thong or panty lines.

The sexual tension was building and Terra felt herself getting moist with every word he spoke. "Nothing. Just the dress."

"So, if I reached my hand underneath your dress right at this very moment, I would feel nothing but your sweet wet pussy?"

"And how do you know it's wet?"

"Because my dick is like a Geiger counter, and gets hard once it detects heat from a wet pussy," he said, ever so slowly lifting the hem of her dress.

"So your dick is hard?" she asked, moving her hips into his rising erection.

"As Chinese arithmetic." Mason rubbed her smooth outer thigh, moved his hand around to her ass, and softly rubbed each cheek. He watched Terra close her eyes, and knew she was putty in his hands. He was slowly seducing her and though he was enjoying every minute of their verbal foreplay, he was ready to feel his dick inside of her warm pussy before he exploded inside his pants.

"I'm really good at math," she said, opening her lustful eyes.

Mason moved one hand around to her manicured triangle, found her clit, and began stroking the tiny piece of flesh with his index finger. "How good?"

"Good enough to solve this extremely hard problem," she said, reaching down and massaging his balls and firm cock.

Her touch almost made him cum right then and there, but he restrained himself. Instead, he scooped her into his arms and carried her into the bedroom. The room was dark, except for the glow of the streetlights streaming through the slits of the miniblinds. Before laying her on top of the comforter, Mason pulled the dress over her head, exposing her perfect body. He then took off his jeans, underwear, and T-shirt, and laid his naked body next to hers.

Mason's eyes traveled the length of her body from the curls in her hair to the polish on her toes. He drank in her beauty like a man dying of thirst. He lightly ran the palm of his hand over her honey-dipped skin. "I love you, Terra." He finally verbalized the words that were in his heart from the first day he laid eyes on her.

"I love you too, Mason," she confessed, to him as well as to herself.

Her words reverberated through his mind, drowning out the unsavory thoughts of Rico and his blackmail scheme. Mason was happier than he'd ever been in his life, and he wanted to savor every second of his newfound bliss, so he dismissed his plan to tell Terra about his past and instead made love to her, because at the moment that was the only thing that mattered.

22

TERRA WAS viewing life through rose-colored glasses, and everything and everyone seemed more vibrant and alive than the day before. After making love with Mason the entire night, she felt a renewed sense of purpose, and the second she got home from his apartment the next day, she called her agent.

"Hi, FK, it's Terra," she said, once the assistant put her through.

"Well, hello, I haven't heard from you since you blew the Dove audition," Feodora said, without mincing her words. It was Feodora's policy that her clients call in after an audition to let her know how the reading went. If the audition was a success, the wannabe actors would call her bubbling over with confidence that they had nailed the part, but if they bombed, she wouldn't hear from them for weeks.

"I know I should have called you, but I've been so preoccupied lately," she said, thinking of Mason. "Anyway, I was calling to have you set me up with a screen test. I'm tired of going on go-sees, and

I'm ready to audition for a juicy movie role," she informed her agent, using the clout that her last name bought her.

"This must be your lucky day. I just got off the phone with Searchlight, and they're casting for an upcoming urban romance film. If you're interested, I'll messenger over a copy of the script. The reading is tomorrow, so you'll have plenty of time to memorize your lines." Feodora knew that Terra wasn't the most talented actress in her stable, but she was the richest, so she tossed her a bone every now and then—not that she expected Terra to catch it—to keep her happy. Besides, it enhanced her agency's profile to have an heiress on the roster.

"Thanks, FK, and I promise I'm going to nail it this time," she reassured her agent.

"Let's hope so. By the way, what's happening with the studio Sage Hirschfield is building? I've called around and the only thing I found out is that he bought an old soundstage in Long Island City and is having it renovated."

Terra didn't have any information. Sage was being so close-mouthed about his plans that she had no idea when the studio would be up and running. After boasting about Sage being an old family friend, she was embarrassed to tell Feodora that she was totally clueless. "I talked to him the other day and he said the renovations are taking longer than he expected," she said, lying to save face.

"Well, keep me updated on the studio's progress since you have the inside track. And you can expect the script within the hour," Feodora said, and hung up.

Sure enough, sixty minutes later, a messenger delivered the script with a note from Feodora telling Terra which part to study. Terra dove right into the story and read the screenplay from beginning to end, to get a feel for the movie—which was a cross between *The Best Man* and *G*—before she began rehearsing her lines. The part she was reading for wasn't the main character, but she didn't mind because her character was a feisty, around the way girl from the Bronx, which was in sharp contrast to herself. Terra had worked with a dialect coach before so she knew how to change her proper speaking voice into that distinctive, boogie-down Bronx tone. She read and reread her lines until three o'clock in the morning. When she was confident that she knew every single word, she turned off the lights and went to bed.

The next morning, Terra dressed the part of Roxanne, a smart-talking tomboy, and put on a pair of tight jeans, a midriff shirt, a pair of Timberlands, and stuffed her hair underneath a Yankees baseball cap. Even though the script didn't call for it, she decided to chew a wad of bubble gum to help bring the character to life. Terra called Leroy and told him to pick her up at eleven-thirty. The audition was at one and she didn't want to be late. On the ride downtown, she rehearsed her lines again, because she didn't want a reoccurrence of the Dove audition, when she flubbed her lines three times. Today, she had the dialogue down cold and had no intention of blowing the screen test.

Unlike the hordes of women waiting their turn in front of the camera at the Dove soap commercial, there was no one there other than the receptionist when she stepped off the elevator. She walked over to the desk and introduced herself.

"Go right on in, Ms. Benson. The casting director is ready for you," the receptionist said, pointing to the door across from her desk.

Terra loved this civilized method, much better than the chaotic cattle call. She reached into her tote, took out two pieces of Dubble Bubble, unwrapped the pink thick pieces, and stuck the gum in her mouth. Now she was ready, and was calm and collected when she entered the room. "Hi. I'm Terra Benson," she said, shaking the director's hand.

He took in her appearance and nodded with approval. "I see you got the look of Roxanne down cold. Now let's see how you translate that to film. I'm going to read the part of Jessica, her best friend." He flipped through the script. "Let's start at the top of page one-o-six, the scene where Roxanne is trying to talk Jessica out of marrying Enrique."

Terra knew exactly what scene he was taking about, and had the lines completely memorized. "Jessica, yew know as well as I do dat Enrique ain't no good for yew," she said in a heavy Bronx accent.

"But I love him, Rox," the casting director said.

"What yew love about him? He's a playa wit women in every borough."

"He told me that his playing days are over."

"And yew believe dat?" Terra was nailing the lines, and started smacking on the gum to really bring Roxanne to life.

"Why shouldn't I believe him?"

" 'Cuz." She blew a huge bubble and popped it. "He ain't nothin' but a user who just wants yew fo yo money," she said, popping another bubble.

"Cut!" said the director. "Where'd the gum come from? It's distracting. Take it out."

Terra was caught completely off guard. She thought the gum was a good prop; it was helping her get into character. She didn't want to argue with him, so she removed the wad of gum and continued with her lines. "Enrique hasn't had a job in two years, and ..."

"Cut!" the director yelled. "What happened to your Bronx accent? The line is supposed to be, 'Enrique ain't had no job in two years.' "

Terra didn't realize that she'd dropped the accent, and tried to pick it back up, but the director's yelling was beginning to make her nervous. "Okay, got it."

"Take three," he said before she began again.

"Enrique ain't had no job in two years," she said with an accent.

"Cut! What type of accent is that?"

"It's a Bronx accent," she said sheepishly.

"Bronx by way of Boston. It's more Boston than Bronx, which isn't good, since the movie takes place uptown. Okay, it was great meeting you. I'll have my assistant call your agent," he said, abruptly ending the screen test.

"Wait a minute. Give me one more chance. I know the lines," she pleaded.

"It's not the lines I'm worried about, it's the accent, and I'm afraid you just don't have it down cold," he said bluntly.

She took his criticism like a pro, thanked him for the opportunity, and left. Terra couldn't believe she had blown another audition. She needed to land a part and soon before FK dropped her from the roster. At this point, her only saving grace was Sage. If only he would agree to give her a chance. Then she could tell her agent that she had landed a starring role in a major production. Terra was at a crossroads and had to come up with a solution and quick.

"Leroy, drop me off at the Hirschfield building," she told her driver the second she got in the car.

On the way over to Sage's office, Terra thought about her foiled attempt at seducing him. Maybe if she had slept with him a few months ago when he was after her, then she wouldn't be in the position of having to beg him to star in one of his films. Now that she was in love with Mason, sleeping with Sage wasn't an option any longer. Her best bet at this point was to try to appeal to his sensitive side and hope that he would feel sorry for her and give her a much needed break.

23

SAGE HAD been in secretarial hell for the past two weeks. Pearl had been hospitalized with a serious case of influenza and now she was at home recuperating. Being the ever-efficient assistant that she was, Pearl called daily to check in, and Sage reassured her that everything at the office was under control and running smoothly. He lied through his teeth during every call, but he didn't want her to worry; he just wanted her to hurry up and recover so that she could come back and rescue him from the stream of incompetent temps. One temp was worse than the others and he was at his wit's end; they couldn't keep his schedule straight let alone construct a proper letter. The only thing they were useful for was running errands, and even then he had to give explicit instructions and write a note for a coffee run, so the order wouldn't be screwed up.

"Mr. Hirschfield, a Mr. Snyderman is here to see you," the temp said, poking her head through his office door.

Sage was on the phone with his attorney, and held up his index finger, indicating that she should wait a minute. "Okay, Bob. Yes, that sounds great. I'll keep an eye out for that contract. Okay, talk to you soon," he said, hanging up.

"Come in for a second." He waved her over. Once she was standing in front of his desk, Sage handed her a pink slip of paper. "I need for you to pick up my dry cleaning. The address of the cleaners is on the top of the ticket, and on your way back, bring two double espressos with a little skim milk in both." He scribbled down the order on his memo pad, tore off the small sheet of paper, and handed it to her. "Thanks, Lucy. You can send in Mr. Snyderman now."

Sage hadn't seen Roy since their naughty sexcapade with Lena. He'd kept his self-imposed vow and remained extremely professional during their many telephone calls regarding the studio. The final plans had been approved and the renovation was back on schedule. Today Sage was meeting with Roy to choose paint colors, light fixtures, flooring, and furniture for the executive offices within the studio. Though Roy was an architect, his company had an in-house interior design department and he oversaw the projects of his A-list clients, and Hirschfield Multimedia was at the top of that list.

"How's it going, Roy?" Sage asked, shaking the architect's hand.

"It's going great. I've been busier than a worker bee. Just got back from the West Coast yesterday," he said, walking into the office and closing the door behind him.

"Busy's better than being idle." Sage got up from his desk and went over to the mini conference table.

"This is true. Keeps me out of trouble," Roy said, cutting his eyes at Sage and slightly raising his left brow.

Sage took one look at the sly expression on Roy's face and knew that he was thinking about the unexpected blow job at Lena's apartment. Men gave the best head and Sage couldn't help but smile at the memory of that delicious surprise. "Some of us love trouble," Sage shot back.

Roy set the bag of color swatches, catalogues, and flooring samples on the oval table and stood directly in front of Sage. "Did you know my middle name is trouble?" he asked, taking Sage's cue and running his hand up and down the lapel on Sage's gabardine suit jacket.

Sage knew that he was treading in dangerous waters flirting with Roy, but their cat and mouse game was thrilling and making the hairs on the back of his neck stand on end. He should have stopped Roy from going further, but his dick had already responded to Roy's seductive words and was growing harder by the second. *I could use a quick blow job. Besides, the silly temp is out on an errand, and no one is in the outer office,* he thought, trying to justify breaking his self-imposed vow.

Sage took a step closer. "Is that trouble with a capital 'T'?"

"A capital 'T' and double 'b,' " he said, sliding his hand from Sage's lapel down to his belt buckle.

"What's the extra 'b' for?" Sage asked suggestively.

Roy unbuckled Sage's belt, unzipped his pants, and flipped his swollen cock out through the zipper. "For Big." He rubbed his hand along the length of Sage's shaft. "And I must say, you have one of the biggest cocks I've ever seen. The head is so full and round that I'm just dying to suck it again." He caressed the circumference. "You don't mind, do you?" he asked rhetorically, dropping to his knees without waiting for an answer.

Sage unbuttoned his pants and took them off, along with his boxer briefs, backed up slightly, sat on the edge of the conference table, and cocked his legs wide open to give easier access. "Be my guest."

Roy flicked out his tongue and licked Sage's balls before putting the entire scrotum in his mouth; he sucked the meaty sack until Sage squirmed with pleasure. He then took his right hand and guided Sage's long rod inside of his mouth. Roy began sucking both his dick and balls at the same time, while lightly fingering his ass.

"Oh . . . shit . . . you . . . got . . . mad skills," Sage gasped. He had never had his balls and dick sucked simultaneously and the sensation was orgasmic. He didn't want to come just yet, because he was enjoying the hell out of Roy's oral dexterity, so he closed his eyes to concentrate on staying hard.

Roy grabbed the cheeks of Sage's naked ass and pulled him off of the table and closer to him, so that Sage's dick was nearly down his throat. He had given so many blow jobs in his life that his gag reflexes were permanently numb, so he didn't choke like most women did when a dick hit the back of their tonsils. He deep-throated Sage until he tasted the salty semen leaking out of his tiny slit, then sucked even harder to extract more of the tasty cum. They were so wrapped up giving and receiving pleasure that they didn't hear the door quietly open.

"OHMYGOD!!"

Sage's eyes popped open, but Roy kept sucking. He was in a zone and oblivious to the sudden interruption. "Uhh . . . uhh . . ." Sage stuttered, and tried to extract his dick from Roy's mouth, but the suction was too tight. "TERRA, what are you doing here!?"

Her eyes were glued to the back of Roy's head bobbing up and down on Sage's dick. "Your secretary wasn't at her desk, so I just came in," she said in a low monotone voice, as if in shock. "Guess, I came at the wrong time," she said, still staring at Roy slobbering all over Sage's cock.

"Terra, it's not—" Before he could finish his sentence she had rushed out of the office, slamming the door shut behind her. "FUCK!" Sage screamed at the top of his lungs.

Hearing that four-letter word, Roy stopped sucking, wiped his mouth with his monogrammed shirt sleeve, got up off his knees, and said, "You want to be the fucker or the fuckee?"

Sage snatched his pants and underwear off the floor and quickly put them on. "Roy, this meeting is over. You have to leave right now," he said, buckling his belt and hastily tucking his shirttail into the waistband of his pants.

"What's the matter? Didn't you like the dual action B.J.?" he asked, confused as to why Sage had suddenly switched gears.

"Didn't you hear my friend walk in on us?"

"Yeah, I did. But your juices were just beginning to flow and I didn't want to stop. You were tasting so good. Besides, what was the use in stopping at that point? She had already walked in on us. Who was that anyway?"

"My friend Terra," Sage said nervously.

"Is that your girlfriend?" Roy asked nonchalantly.

"No, not really."

"Then what's the problem?"

Sage began pacing in front of his desk. He didn't know how he could explain getting his dick sucked by another man without sounding gay or bisexual. "The problem is she knows my family extremely well, and I can't risk her telling my father what she just walked in on."

"You really think she'd go running to your old man? Anyway, so what if she did? You are the CEO of this conglomerate, not your father."

"It's more complicated than that. Even though my father is retired, he's still the majority stockholder and can replace me at his discretion. My dad is from the old school and extremely traditional. He's been on my back lately about getting married, so if he found out I was a liberal lover, he'd be morally disappointed and would probably disinherit me. I don't own Hirschfield Publishing or Hirschfield Multimedia outright like you own your company, so you see I have more at stake than you do."

"I feel for you." Roy shook his head. "I'm glad my fate isn't in the hands of anyone but the big guy upstairs," he said, straightening his clothes before gathering his belongings.

Sage walked Roy to the door. "I don't think we should have another face-to-face meeting. It's just too risky. Next time, send over one of your associates. Once this project is complete, maybe we can hang out at Lena's sometime."

"No problem," Roy said, and opened the door to leave.

Sage looked into the outer office and couldn't believe his eyes. There, standing at the secretary's desk, was his father, talking to Terra. From where he stood, he couldn't hear what they were saying, but only hoped it wasn't his worst nightmare come true. He quickly shot Roy a look that read "get out of here."

Roy briskly brushed past Terra and the elder Hirschfield without saying a word and made a beeline straight to the bank of elevators.

Terra looped her arm through Mr. Hirschfield's and walked toward Sage. "I was just telling your father . . ."

Sage's vision began to get blurry and his ears started ringing. Hearing the beginning of her sentence, it sounded like she had already blurted out his dirty secret, and Sage thought that he was about to faint, but her next words brought him back to life.

". . . that we had such a great time at Chanterelle, and what a beautiful pearl necklace you gave me for graduation," she said, smiling like nothing was out of order.

"That's my boy." He slapped his son on the back with fatherly pride. "Exquisite food and exquisite jewelry. I taught him well. And now he has an exquisite woman," he said, looking from Terra to Sage. "So, you two, when are you going to make it official?" he asked, totally out of left field.

Sage was afraid to make eye contact with Terra, so he turned around toward the door. "Come on. Let's go into my office," he said, avoiding the question and ushering them inside. "The temp should be back any minute with Starbucks," he said, trying to make small talk.

Henry Hirschfield sat on the tufted leather sofa and patted the cushion next to him. "Sit here, Terra, and tell me, when are you going to marry my handsome son?"

After witnessing Sage getting his dick sucked by another man, Terra was repulsed. In her mind, men on the down low were sleazy, in public they wanted to front with beautiful women, but in private they wanted to butt-fuck other men. Her initial thought was to out Sage, but she knew that information would destroy his father, so she used her acting skills instead. She smiled and said, "Mr. Hirschfield, we're both too young to be getting married. There's plenty of time for white lace and wedding cake."

"Fiddlesticks! When I was your age, I was married with a family." He shook his head. "I just don't understand you young folks today."

"Dad, don't put Terra on the spot," Sage said, coming to her rescue. "Anyway, I'm sure she didn't come here to talk about marriage and babies."

Terra got up to leave. "As a matter of fact, I'm late for an appointment," she said, glancing down at her silver Rolex. "Give me a call later, Sage, so we can talk."

That was one conversation that he was dreading. "Okay," he said, and walked her to the door.

"So what brings you by?" he asked his father once Terra was gone.

"I read the latest quarterly statements and since you've been in charge, our earnings have increased across the board. And it's all due to you breathing fresh new ideas into this old company. Like

your idea to expand into the movie industry. I think that was ge-
nius. Since there are very few soundstages located in New York,
we'll have a major foothold on the East Coast. Son, I just can't tell
you how proud I am of you."

Sage glanced over at the conference table where only a few
minutes ago he was getting his dick sucked by another man. If his
father had walked in instead of Terra, this conversation would have
a totally different slant. He silently thanked his lucky stars and returned his focus back to his father who was still singing his praises.

MASON WAS in his office crunching numbers on his calculator. He should've been calculating vendor invoices, payroll, and new membership numbers, but he was busy dissecting his personal finances. After hearing Terra say that she loved him, he couldn't risk telling her the truth—even love had its limits—and he knew his past would be a deal breaker. Terra was extremely private and wouldn't want her name associated with a seedy blackmail scheme, which was sure to be splashed all over the tabloids, if the secret was ever exposed. So, Mason was willing to do whatever it took to keep those pictures and videos from ever seeing the light of day, and that included emptying his bank account and borrowing against his condo. He had saved over two hundred thousand dollars for med school, but his relationship with Terra was more important than going back to school. He didn't have much equity in his condo, since he had recently bought it, and could only borrow fifty thousand, but he wouldn't get that money for another week. He was short three-quarters of a million dollars, and had no way of coming up with the rest of the money. Mason leaned down and began slowly banging his forehead on top of the desk out of desperation. He thought about going down to Mexico and selling a kidney, but the way his luck was running, he'd probably end up gutted on some butcher's table, never to be seen or heard from again.

"Whoa there, you're going to break the desk if you keep that up," Trey said, walking into the office and watching Mason assault the furniture.

Mason raised his head and had a forlorn expression plastered across his face. He wasn't expecting Trey and was caught off guard. He was feeling lower than low and hated to be seen at his worst, but Trey was not only his boss, he was a friend, and true friends understood moments like this. "Hey, man," he finally said.

"Yo, dude, what's up with you? You look like your puppy died." Trey chuckled, trying to make Mason laugh, but his joke didn't work, because Mason didn't crack a smile.

"I wish it were that simple; then I'd just get a new puppy. But this is way more serious," he said, holding his head in his hands.

Trey sat down in front of Mason's desk and asked in a sincere voice, "What's the matter?"

Mason didn't know where to start. There was no way he was going to tell Trey about his homosexual indiscretion back in college. He wasn't gay or bisexual, or on the DL like some men. He never even fucked Rico. He just let the little faggot give him some head a few times, when his girlfriend wasn't around and he was feeling horny. Now, his lack of good judgment as a teen was coming back to haunt him as a man. If only he'd kept his hormones in check—then and now—then none of this would be happening. But without telling Trey about Rico, how could he tell him about the blackmail scheme? "Trust me, this is one story you don't want to hear."

"Try me. Being in this business, I've heard just about everything under the sun, so nothing you say can surprise me," he said, reassuring his friend.

Even though Trey sounded convincing, some things needed to be left unsaid, and having his dick sucked by another man was one of them. "Let's just say, I've got women trouble."

"Now that's my specialty," Trey said, pulling his chair closer to the desk and resting his elbows on the edge. "Does this have anything to do with Ms. Benson? I remember you telling me that she was 'the one.' Don't tell me she's broken your heart already."

"No, man, she's in love with me," he said. Mason could still hear those three little words she whispered to him, and instantly a smile brightened his face.

"If you love her and she loves you, then what's the problem? She's not engaged to be married to someone else, is she?" he asked, thinking about his own sordid past.

Mason's smile quickly faded. "No, it's nothing like that." Mason wished that was his problem. Another man he could deal with, but being blackmailed was in an entirely different league, an area in which he had no prior experience.

"Okay, now you've got me stumped. Come on, man, tell me, because I'm tired of guessing."

"Let's just say, I've got to pay off a lowlife photographer, or else he's going to give the tabloids plenty of material to print in their rags," he said, his somber tone returning.

"How much?"

Mason didn't want to tell Trey that the ransom for the pictures was one million dollars, because he knew an amount that huge would raise more questions, and he'd shared all that he was willing to share, so he just said, "More than I got."

"Sorry to hear that, man. I guess dating an heiress isn't as glamorous as it sounds. With the paparazzi hounding her down, I'm sure it's hard to have any privacy."

"Yeah, it's tough," Mason agreed, even though that wasn't the problem either. He could dodge paparazzi, but he couldn't dodge Rico.

"Well, this must be your lucky day, because the reason I came by was to give you this," he said, handing Mason a white envelope.

"What is it?"

"A bonus. Since you've been managing the downtown club, membership has nearly doubled. You keep inventing new theme rooms that the clients love and the word of mouth is spreading like wildfire. The Black Door is so popular with the ladies that I'm going to have to open a club in every major city across America." Trey beamed like a proud papa ready to procreate another offspring.

"Thanks, Trey, this couldn't have come at a better time."

"You deserve it, you're an awesome manager. Now, I've got to run. I have a lunch meeting uptown with an architectural firm to check out their portfolio. If they're good, I'll let you know so we can meet with them regarding designing the new theme room," Trey said, getting up to leave. He walked to the door, and then turned around. "Keep your head up. I'm sure everything will work out fine."

"From your mouth to God's ears," Mason said solemnly.

Once Trey was gone, Mason tore open the envelope and took out his bonus, which was a check for twenty-five thousand dollars. Any other time he would have been ecstatic about getting unexpected money, but this wouldn't even put a dent in his deficit. He folded the check, put it in his shirt pocket, went into the closet, took out his backpack, and left the office.

It was nearly three o'clock, so Mason jogged four blocks to the bank before it closed. He filled out a withdrawal slip and stood in line. As he waited his turn, he glanced down at the amount on the paper, and couldn't believe that he was getting ready to take out his hard-earned savings and hand it over to that scum Rico. This money was earmarked for his education. Now it would probably be used to cut off Rico's dick and construct a fake pussy. *What a freak of nature*, Mason thought, and made his way to the window.

"How may I help you today?" asked the teller.

"I'd like to make a withdrawal, and I'd like to cash this check."

She looked at the amount on the withdrawal slip. "For an amount this large, you'll have to see one of our personal bankers."

Mason walked in the direction of where the personal bankers sat. He had a personal banker, but the situation with Rico had his mind twisted and he wasn't thinking straight, that's why he walked directly to the teller initially. "I need to make a withdrawal," Mason told the banker, once he sat down.

"Sure, I can help you with that. Can I see your driver's license?"

Mason reached in his wallet and handed over his identification.

After typing Mason's information into the system, the banker asked, "How much would you like to withdraw today, Mr. Anthony?"

"Two hundred thousand."

The banker looked shocked. "Mr. Anthony, that'll only leave you with a hundred dollars in your account. Are you sure you want to make such a large withdrawal?" he quizzed Mason.

"Yes," he said simply, without offering an explanation. It was his money, and he didn't feel the need to explain why he wanted his cash.

"Oh, I see. Would you like that in a cashier's check?"

"No. Cash."

"Oh." The banker's face registered another shocked expression. He typed an approval code in the computer, and then said, "You can go back to the teller, and she'll be happy to count out your money. Have a nice day, Mr. Anthony."

His day was turning out to be anything but nice. Mason nodded his head in response and returned to the teller. He told her he wanted large and small bills. Mason figured that a backpack full of cash would look more enticing than a check for a quarter of what Rico was demanding. Since the funds from his condo wouldn't be available for another week, he had to make the backpack look like it was bursting with money.

The teller counted out two hundred twenty-five thousand dollars, and he put the bundles of cash in his backpack. With only one hundred dollars left in his savings account, Mason felt like a broke loser.

Outside, he took Rico's card out of his back pocket, flipped open his cell phone, and made the dreaded call.

"Hello?" purred a female voice on the other end.

Mason was caught totally off guard and asked, "Rico, is that you?"

"I told you, my name is Missy now," she snapped, changing her demure tone into a harsher one.

"Whatever, dude," Mason said, purposely referring to Missy as a man.

"I hope you didn't call to insult me. I hope you're calling because you have a cashier's check for me," she said, her voice turning soft again.

"I have something better than a cashier's check. I have cash," he said, as if he had the entire amount. "And it's all for you, on one condition," Mason said, laying down the rules and taking control of the situation.

Missy's ears perked up. Cash was right up her alley. Now there would be no paper trail with the bank. She could put the money in a safe deposit box and access it anytime she wanted without the government ever knowing that she was a millionaire. "I'm listening."

"First, I want you to gather the videos, the pictures, and the negatives, and put them in a bag. Then I want you to type a letter saying that any photographs or video of Terra Benson or Mason Anthony taken by Rico Sanns or Missy whatever your last name is have been digitally altered and are fake, not to be used by any publication or shown on any entertainment show. Then I want you to have the letter notarized, and when we make the trade-off, I want the evidence along with the note. Is that clear?"

Missy thought about it for a minute, weighing her options. She didn't like the idea of signing her name in front of a notary public and admitting that the pictures were bogus, but on the other hand, with a million dollars, she could get her operation, quit dancing, buy the condo that she lived in, and finally become a lady of leisure. "Okay, you got a deal," she said, agreeing to his terms.

"Meet me at eight o'clock in the lobby of the Soho Grand and don't be late," Mason said sternly.

"I'll be there. Just have my money," Missy said, and hung up.

Mason made a beeline home, unwrapped the bundles of cash, and dumped the money back into the backpack. With the bills loose, it looked like some serious loot and it was hard to see at first glance how much money was actually in the bag. His plan was to give Rico the backpack, take the notarized letter, and get the hell out of the hotel before Rico had a chance to count the money and realize that he had been gypped. Now if the plan worked, Mason would be home free, but if it didn't, he was screwed.

SAGE STILL couldn't believe that he'd been busted by Terra. He should have never broken his vow and let Roy go down on him, but his dick had overruled his senses and had gotten him in trouble. This wasn't the first time that his libido had led him down the wrong path. It had all started the night he met Missy.

Sage and some of his old college buddies were having a bachelor party at Scores. They were celebrating impending nuptials and buying bottles of champagne like beer, and drinking them down just as fast. The bubbly was making them frisky, and the beautiful women dancing onstage were making the men's dicks hard.

"She's gorgeous," the groom-to-be said, pointing to a brunette with tassels dangling off the nipples of her petite boobs.

"Cute face, but her titties are too small for me," Sage commented.

"They're small, but look at her ass. It's so big and juicy that it makes Jennifer Lopez's ass look as flat as a pancake," he said, licking his lips in lust.

"I'm a breast man myself, and she has just the type of titties I'd love to suck," Sage said, referring to a stripper with humongous, football-size boobs. He couldn't take his eyes off her as she got down on her hands and knees and crawled like a black panther across the stage. Her titties were so big that her firm dark nipples nearly brushed the floor with every stealthlike move. Sage could feel an erection coming on as he watched her titties sway from side to side. Once the song was finished, he motioned her over for a lap dance.

"What can I do for you, Big Daddy?" she asked, standing directly in front of him.

Sage stared at her naked breasts, which were right near his mouth. They looked so luscious that he wanted to stick his tongue out and suck her nipples until she came, but touching the dancers wasn't allowed. "You can start by giving me a lap dance." He smiled.

She straddled him without hesitating, and began grinding on his hard cock to the beat of the music. She took her hands and started playing with her nipples, making them extra hard, and then brushed them across his lips.

Instinctively, Sage stuck out his tongue and quickly licked her nipples before any of the bouncers saw him. She was teasing him so good and making him so hot that he nearly came in his underwear. "You're one sexy woman. What's your name?"

"Missy," she whispered in his ear. "What's yours?"

Even her husky voice was sexy and turned him on more. "I'm Sage. Can I see you later tonight, Missy?" he asked, wasting no time with useless chitchat.

Missy looked at the bottles of expensive champagne littering their table and quickly surmised that these men were high rollers.

The markup on the liquor was astronomical, but obviously they didn't have a problem paying hundreds of dollars for a bottle of champagne. "Sure, but I don't get off until late."

"Not a problem. I'll be waiting out front in a black BMW 7 Series."

By the time Sage and his friends left the club, they were flying high and feeling no pain. They said good night and went their separate ways. Sage got in his car and parked a few feet from the entrance. He turned the music up while he waited. The combination of the jazzy saxophone playing in the background and the liquor flowing through his veins was making him horny all over again, so he released his captive dick, which had been dying to get free all night, and started rubbing the swollen head. A light tap on the window interrupted him, and he looked through the tinted windows and saw that it was Missy. Sage didn't bother putting his dick away; he just hit the automatic locks and opened the door.

She slid into the plush leather passenger seat. "Is that for me?" she asked, looking down at his erect cock.

"If you want it," he said, still rubbing the bulbous head.

Missy didn't say a word, she just leaned over, covered his dick with her mouth, and began sucking him feverishly up and down. He was already hard, and it didn't take long to get him to explode inside her mouth. Missy got off on sucking dick and loved to see the shocked expression on most guys' faces when she swallowed their creamy cum without hesitation. "Does that answer your question?" she said, sitting up.

"Damn, Baby, that was good. Now open your coat and let me see those beautiful tits."

Missy took off her trench coat. Underneath, she wore a sheer blouse, a lacy bra, and a pair of snug, low-cut jeans. She slowly unbuttoned each button like she was putting on a private strip show, and then took her titties out and let them rest on top of the bra cups. "Are these what you want to see?" she asked, running her hands across each swollen breast.

Sage reached over and began fondling her boobs, something he had wanted to do all night. "Your titties are so big that I could feast on them until the sun comes up."

"What the hell are you waiting for?" she asked, moving her body closer to his. "Feast away."

He buried his head in between each gigantic titty and started sucking from one to the other. They were so delicious, just like he imagined. His dick was getting hard again, and now he wanted to fuck. Sage reached for the zipper on her jeans, but she put a hand on top of his and stopped him.

"Just so you know, I only like anal sex," she whispered.

Sage couldn't believe his ears. The women he'd been with hated anal sex and he had to beg just to finger their ass. "Come on. Let's get in the backseat." He was so horny that he couldn't wait any longer. He had to fuck her right then before she changed her mind.

Missy climbed in the back first, took off her jeans, but left on her thong. She moved the thin piece of fabric to the side, got on her knees with her ass high in the air, and said, "Come on, Big Daddy. Let me see what you got."

Sage followed right behind her. He wedged open her cheeks and eased the head of his dick into her tiny asshole. Once the rim of his head was in, he grabbed her hips, pulled her to him, and slid the rest of his long rod deep into the recesses of her ass. Her sphincter muscle gripped his dick tightly as he plunged in and out.

"Oh, yes, Daddy, fuck that hole," she moaned.

"You like that, Bitch?" He slapped the side of her thigh.

"I love it. Just don't stop fucking me, Motherfucker."

Sage closed his eyes and fucked her strong for a straight ten minutes until he saw stars. He came so hard up her ass that he thought his sperm would come shooting out of her mouth. Sage had never had anal sex like that before and became addicted to Missy. On the days that he couldn't see her, he'd call her and they would have heated phone sex.

It wasn't until two months after he'd been fucking her that he found out about her extra appendage. Missy always insisted on keeping her thong on during sex, which didn't bother Sage, because that thin strip of material never got in his way. But one night he was fucking her so hard up the ass that the strap broke, and when it did, her tiny penis dropped out. It was dark in the room, and Sage thought that he was seeing things.

"What the hell is that!?"

Missy pulled the covers over her embarrassing male anatomy. "I have a penis," she said softly.

"Were you born with male and female parts?" he asked, still trying to comprehend what was going on.

"No." She dropped her head. "I was born male on the outside, but since I was a little boy, I've felt like a girl inside. I've been going through the process of becoming a full-fledged woman, and now the only other operation I need is to have my penis removed and a vagina constructed."

Sage was speechless. He had never been with a man before and didn't have any homosexual desires. He was confused. In his mind, he'd been fucking a woman. Even though he loved anal sex, he didn't think that this made him gay, because he still loved pussy.

"Say something," Missy said, looking at the blank expression on his face.

"When are you getting the operation?"

"As soon as I save the rest of the money. Insurance doesn't cover the costs and it's extremely expensive," she explained.

Sage reasoned that once she got the operation, she would have everything that a real woman had except reproductive organs. He thought about not seeing her until the operation was complete, but he was addicted to her ass and the way she gave head, and didn't want to stop having sex on a technicality. Fucking Missy opened a whole new world to him, and now he wasn't opposed to having a man suck his dick. He never reciprocated because he couldn't imagine going down on another guy. So as far as he was concerned, he wasn't gay or bisexual. He was just liberal.

He was certain that Terra wouldn't see it that way. He was embarrassed and didn't want to have to explain why a man was sucking his dick, but he had to tell her something. He reluctantly picked up the phone and made the dreaded call.

"Hello?"

"Hey, Terra, how are you?"

"Fine. How are things with you?" she asked with a hint of sarcasm in her voice.

Sage could tell by her tone that she was referring to the scene in his office. He decided to get right to the point and not beat around the bush. "Terra, what you walked in on the other day isn't what you think. First of all, I'm not gay—"

"Then why was another man sucking your dick?"

Sage realized that no matter how he tried to spin it, the fact was that he was caught in a homosexual act. "It's a long story," he said, preferring not to go into his history with Missy. "The reason why I'm calling is to thank you for not letting my father walk in on us. If he'd seen me and Roy, there's no telling what he would have done. Look, I owe you big-time." Sage knew that he needed more than an apology to keep his secret safe. "And to show my appreciation for your discretion, I'm going to sign you to a two-picture contract."

Terra couldn't believe her ears. She was finally going to star in a big budget production, and she didn't have to sleep with him or beg. All it took was her catching Sage with his pants down. "Oh, Sage, thank you so much, and I promise I won't let you down."

"I know you won't. After watching you handle my father like nothing had ever happened between me and Roy, I saw firsthand what a good actress you are. I'll have my attorney draw up the contract immediately and have it sent over to your agent."

"Sage, I can't tell you how much this means to me. Thank you again."

"No problem, and just remember that what happened the other day stays between us. No one ever needs to know," he said, making sure that she understood the terms of their deal.

"Don't worry, Sage, your secret is safe with me. I'll talk to you soon," she said, and hung up.

Sage leaned back in his chair and breathed a sigh of relief. He knew that he could trust Terra, because being an actress was more important to her than outing him to his father. Fortunately his dad adored Terra and wouldn't question his decision to work with a close friend, especially once he saw her talent. His father didn't like nepotism, but if a person was well qualified for the job he would make an exception, and that day in his office Terra had proven herself to be a skilled actress.

26

MISSY'S PAYDAY had finally arrived and she was thrilled beyond belief. She had already called and made an appointment to see the surgeon who would perform the sex change operation. Now she'd be able to throw out her wardrobe of extra small thongs that had kept her package in place all of these years. Her next call was to her real estate broker, to inform her that she finally had the cash for a substantial down payment for the apartment that she lived in. With real estate prices out the wazoo, and the six-figure cost of the reconstruction, Missy's funds were dwindling before she even had her hands on the cash. After paying for the operation and buying the condo, she would barely have five hundred thousand left, and a half million dollars in New York was like having fifty thousand elsewhere, especially with the extravagant way she lived. To secure her financial future, Missy decided to tell Mason that the ransom for the pictures and videos had increased to two million dollars.

Obviously getting his hands on Terra's money was easy, since he'd come up with the initial million with no problems.

Missy went into her closet. Behind her wardrobe of designer clothes was a custom-built safe. She moved the dresses aside to gain access to the combination lock and quickly turned the knob to the left, then to the right, and back to the left, and like magic, the door to the small safe popped open. Inside was her original birth certificate that classified her gender as male, a sapphire and diamond broach from a generous lover, and the incriminating evidence she had on Mason. Missy gathered the videos and pictures and stuffed them into a tote bag. With millions at stake, she decided it would be best to take the evidence out of her home safe and put everything into a more secure safe deposit box at the bank. Her financial freedom was at stake and she wasn't going to take any chances by being careless with the evidence.

Earlier that day, she had typed and printed the letter he requested, had it notarized, and put it in the bag along with the other evidence. She planned to go to the bank first, then meet Mason, show him the notarized letter—to prove that she was serious—and demand a down payment that was sure to be the first of many installments. But she had no intention of giving him the letter until she got more money. Terra was a cash cow, and Missy planned on milking Mason until she had millions stashed away, and then maybe, just maybe, she'd give up the evidence.

Missy took her time showering, dressing, and applying her makeup because she wanted to look flawless. Even though Mason had seen her at the Black Door—scantily dressed—he had never seen her coiffed as the perfect woman. She wanted him to see how attractive she was, and that she was no different from any other woman (especially once she had the operation). It was raining kittens and puppies, so she decided to wear knee-high, black patent leather rain boots, a short black dress, and a white Burberry trench coat. She combed her long hair into a neat chignon, and with her hair pulled back, you could clearly see the one-carat diamond studs in each ear, another gift from a former lover. Missy checked herself in the mirror and had to admit that she looked just like one of those Upper East Side rich bitches who shopped and lunched for a living. A smile slowly crept upon her face at the thought of joining the hordes of women who lived the fabulous life without slaving away at a J.O.B. Yes, she had struck pay dirt and was ready to receive the first of many installments. Missy tied the belt around her waist, threw the tote over her shoulder, grabbed her umbrella, and headed out the door.

By the time she got outside, the rain had increased and now it was pouring cats and dogs. Missy stood underneath the building awning and waited for the doorman to flag down a taxi, but every cab that passed by was occupied. Finding a taxi in New York when it was raining was like trying to find bin Laden in the middle of a sandstorm—nearly impossible—so she decided that her chances would be better if she left the shelter of the awning and scouted a cab for herself. Missy turned up the plaid collar of her coat, popped open the umbrella, and stepped out into the torrential downpour.

Since there were no available taxis in sight, she decided to walk the ten blocks to her bank, deposit the evidence, and then head downtown to meet Mason. The walk took longer than she anticipated and even though her bank stayed open late, by the time she got there it was closed. Missy stood curbside and tried to hail a taxi, but they were either occupied or off duty. She quickly looked at her watch. It was seven-thirty and she was supposed to meet Mason at eight o'clock sharp. She began to panic because she didn't want to be late and risk him walking out of the hotel with her money.

"Damn, I should have called a car service," she mumbled to herself. For a split second, she thought about taking out her cell phone and calling a car, but it was useless, because at this point a car would take at least an hour to arrive and another twenty minutes to take her to SoHo, and by then he would surely be gone.

Missy walked another two blocks before spotting a man across the street getting out of a taxi. Her eyes lit up like bulbs on a Christmas tree, and she jetted across the busy street before someone else hopped in the cab.

She had the umbrella cocked to one side, shielding herself from the rain as she ran, and didn't see that she had stepped directly into the path of an oncoming bus. Before Missy could take another step, she was broadsided and knocked twenty feet in the air. The contents of her tote flew in the air along with her, and as she crashed back to earth in the middle of traffic, the pictures floated down and scattered across the soaking wet pavement.

"Oh, my God! Somebody call an ambulance!" yelled the driver.

When the bus stopped suddenly, it put in motion a horrific chain of events, causing a taxi to swerve up on the sidewalk, nearly killing a crowd of pedestrians, and another bus nearly missed hitting the bumper of the first bus.

Traffic was snarled and backed up for blocks, and by the time the paramedics arrived fifteen minutes later, they took Missy's vital signs, scraped her mangled body off the concrete, placed her on a gurney, and rushed her to the nearest hospital.

MASON ARRIVED at the Soho Grand ten minutes early. The weather was unforgiving. Mother Nature had opened the floodgates, unleashing torrential rains down on the city, so he allowed an extra forty minutes for what was usually a fifteen-minute cab ride. He was nervous about making the exchange, and kept thinking about the possibility of Rico counting the cash right then and there. Mason had a ready-made answer in the event that he did insist. If that was the case, Mason would simply say that counting a million dollars in public wasn't safe. He would make Rico feel so paranoid about carrying that much money that he'd probably run right out of the hotel straight home, before anyone robbed him of his sudden windfall. Mason checked his watch; it was eight o'clock sharp, and he expected Rico to come rushing through the door any minute.

Five minutes later, and Rico still wasn't there. *He probably had a tough time getting a taxi*, Mason thought, knowing what a night-mare it was finding a cab in New York in the rain.

Another two minutes went by, and Mason's cell phone rang. He thought it was Rico calling to say that he was running late, but he looked at the caller ID, and it was Terra. "Hey, sweetheart, how are you?" he asked, after flipping open the phone.

"I'm fantastic! What are you doing? Can you come over? I have some great news to tell you," she said quickly, nearly running her words together.

"Uh, I'm getting ready to go into a meeting, but I can come by later. What's the great news?" Mason wanted to know. He was so wound up that he needed to hear something uplifting as a momentary distraction.

"I'll tell you when you get here," she said, and gave him her address. "Okay, sweetie, I'll see you later."

Hearing the happiness in Terra's voice, Mason began to feel guilty for getting her involved in this mess—even though she knew nothing about the scheme—and would be relieved once the blackmail issue was settled. He took Missy's card out of his pocket and dialed her cell number, but after four rings, the call went to voice mail, and he hung up without leaving a message. He checked his watched again; it was a quarter after eight. He was surprised that Rico wasn't there yet, because he knew how anxious the greedy bastard was to get his hands on the money.

Maybe he's upstairs, Mason thought, and walked up the wrought-iron steps to the lobby bar. The dim lounge area was full of people sipping cocktails and chatting. He squinted his eyes to adjust to the lighting and scanned the plush sofas, but Rico wasn't there. He then walked into the bar area to the left, but he wasn't there either. Mason peeked his head in the restaurant, but still no Rico.

Mason went back downstairs and waited for another thirty minutes. It was nearly nine o'clock, and Rico still hadn't shown his face. All types of thoughts were running through Mason's mind. *Suppose he decided to go straight to Terra and extort the money from her directly?* he thought. But he quickly dismissed that theory, because if that were the case, Terra would've been irate instead of bubbling over with joy when she called. *Maybe he was meeting with a tabloid reporter at this very moment and is showing them the pictures.* But again that didn't make any sense either, since Rico would only be getting a nominal fee for the pictures instead of the million dollars. Mason went through dozens of other scenarios, but none of them made any sense, especially since he told Rico that he had the cash, and there was no way that Rico could have known that Mason didn't have the full amount.

At nine-thirty he decided to leave, because clearly Rico had no intention of showing up. It had stopped raining, and there was a fleet of taxis in front of the hotel. He hopped into one and gave the driver Terra's address. Mason sat in the backseat, freaking out, and didn't know what to do. Rico had changed the rules midgame; now Mason had no clue how to proceed. He took out his phone and redialed Rico's number, but again the call went to voice mail after a few rings. *He's probably looking at the caller ID and purposely ignoring my call.* He wanted to go over to Rico's apartment and confront him, but he didn't know where he lived. The only information on Rico's card was his new name and cell number.

As the taxi cruised up the West Side Highway, Mason carefully weighed his options. On the one hand, he could come clean and tell Terra about his unsavory past and the blackmail scheme, or he could wait until Rico crawled out of the woodwork with the evidence and gave Terra a private viewing of the pornographic videos. Either way, the truth would come out, and Mason knew no matter how hard telling Terra about his homosexual experience would be, she should hear the truth from him. Rico couldn't be trusted and would more than likely spin the facts and paint him to be bisexual, which he wasn't since that was his first and last encounter with a man. As hard as telling her was going to be, Mason knew that he had no other choice.

He wanted to prolong the inevitable for as long as possible, and could have cruised around Manhattan all night, but the driver had pulled in front of her building and was waiting impatiently to get paid. Mason gave him a twenty, told him to keep the change, and got out.

"Mason Anthony to see Ms. Benson," he said to the doorman.

"Go on up, she's expecting you," he said, and gave Mason her apartment number.

"Sweetheart, there's something important I have to tell you," he mumbled in the elevator, trying to rehearse his lines. But no matter what words he used, the truth would sound ugly and disgusting. His only hope was that she could find it in her heart to forgive him. The elevator doors opened, and he slowly stepped off and made his way to her apartment. Doom washed over Mason, as if he were going to face a firing squad, and in a sense he was, because he knew that Terra's eyes would shoot holes through his character the moment she heard the truth. When he reached her door, it was ajar, and he called out her name.

"Come on in, honey, and make a left. I'm in the den!" she yelled.

Mason followed her voice and found her perched on a white leather sofa in an exquisitely decorated room mixed with antiques and sleek Scandinavian furniture. She was watching a plasma television mounted to the wall like a piece of art. "Hey there," he said.

Terra looked over at him and blew him a kiss. "Hey, sweetie." She noticed the backpack swinging off of his left shoulder, smiled, and said, "I see you brought a change of clothes. Now how did you know I was planning a sleepover?" she teased.

"It's not a change of clothes." Mason sat down next to her. "I have something important to tell you."

"So do I. Guess who's going to be starring in a major motion picture? ME!" she blurted out before he had a chance to answer.

"Wow, that's great. When did this happen?" Mason could clearly see that Terra was flying high, and he hated to be the one to let the helium out of her balloon, but it had to be done.

"My friend Sage bought a movie studio and has signed me to a two-picture deal, but I'll tell you all about it in a minute. I want to watch the commercials so I can see who got that Dove commercial that I auditioned for," she said, turning her attention back toward the television.

Mason sat back and waited. After the break was over, the ten o'clock news came back on, and he knew that it was now or never. "Terra, there's something important I have to tell you," he said, moving closer to her.

She looked at Mason and noticed the serious expression on his face. Her heart began to race. She didn't know what he had to say, but whatever it was, it was no laughing matter. In the time that she had known him, she'd never seen him look so somber. "Mason, you're scaring me. What's the matter?"

"It's a long story, so I'll start at the beginning." He took a deep breath. "Back in college——"

"Earlier this evening, in midtown, a bus struck and killed a pedestrian. Witnesses say a woman, later identified as Missy Walker, ran in front of a moving bus and was pronounced dead at St. Vincent's Hospital. The fatal accident caused a major pileup in midtown and tied up traffic for hours," the newscaster said in the background.

The second Mason heard the name Missy Walker, he stopped talking and stared at the screen. The camera crew had obviously arrived after she was taken to the hospital, because there was only a shot of the bus, a ripped tote bag, and debris littering the ground. Mason looked closer at the scene and could see what appeared to be a mangled videotape. Fortunately for him, Missy didn't survive the accident and neither did the evidence. What wasn't destroyed by the rain was crushed underneath the gigantic wheels of the bus. The words "I don't believe it" slipped from his mouth unconsciously.

"Did you know her?" Terra asked, watching the stunned expression on his face.

"No," Mason said, still staring at the screen in disbelief. Now he knew why Rico didn't show up at the hotel. He had been killed by a bus. Mason silently gave homage to whoever or whatever was responsible for ridding the world of Rico. Now there was no need for a full confession, and he wouldn't have to worry about him blackmailing Terra any longer. One crisis was over, but there was still another issue for Mason to deal with. At that moment he decided to wipe the slate clean and tell Terra about his involvement in the Black Door. Which now was the only lie between them, and from this point on, he wanted nothing more to do with half-truths. He took her hand in his. "Sweetheart, remember when we met and I told you I was into real estate?"

"Yes, I remember."

"Well, I'm not. I lied." He waited for her reaction, and when she didn't say anything, he continued. "I manage the downtown location of the Black Door," he said softly, almost in a whisper.

She snatched her hand away from his. "You WHAT!?" she screamed.

"The Black Door, the club that you went to in the Meat-Packing District," he said.

"I know what club you're talking about." She stood up. "Are you telling me that you're the manager of that sleazy sex club?" she said with her hands on her hips.

"It's not sleazy," he said in defense.

"Whatever." She rolled her eyes.

"Will you please sit down and listen to me?"

Instead of sitting next to him on the sofa, Terra crossed the room and sat in a chair. She folded her arms in front of her chest and said, "I'm listening."

Mason told her about his plan of becoming a doctor and working part-time as an escort to help pay for school. He explained that when his funds dried up, he was offered the job of manager at the new club and couldn't say no. With the hefty salary that came with the position, he would be able to save enough money to return to school. He expected Terra to be sympathetic, but she just sat there with her arms crossed, looking pissed. "Come on, Sweetheart, say something," he said, hoping for her forgiveness.

"I'm going to need some time to digest this." Terra couldn't help but think of the press. Starring in a major motion picture would shoot her right to the top of the list of aspiring actresses, and her private life would be dissected more closely now than ever. If the tabloids got wind of her boyfriend operating an erotica club, it would be spread all over the headlines, and her career would be overshadowed by the scandal. She loved Mason, but wasn't ready to sacrifice a lifelong dream that had just come to fruition. "Mason, I think it's best if we cool it for a while."

He was devastated. He didn't think that Terra would end their relationship over his job. It wasn't like the Black Door was illegal, but on the other hand he realized that a woman of her stature couldn't be associated with a profession that could easily be vilified in the press. As he stood up to leave, it occurred to him that if she was putting the breaks on their relationship over his involvement in the Black Door, she would have probably cursed him and ended their relationship flat out if he had told her about Rico. He was grateful that he didn't have to tell her about the blackmail scheme.

Maybe in due time he'd have a chance to salvage their relationship. "I understand."

He ambled toward the doorway with his head hung low, but before he left, he turned around, raised his head, and said, "Terra, just know that I love you, and a love this strong doesn't come along every day." With that said, Mason walked out of her apartment, but prayed to the heavens above that he wasn't walking out of her life for good.

28

"HEY, STRANGER," Lexi said into the phone. She hadn't talked to her friend in nearly a week. "Life on 'Lovers Lane' must be exhausting, with all the good loving that Mason's been laying on you."

"It's not like that at all," Terra said sadly.

"Oh, so you're saying that he ain't rocking your world? Now don't hold back on my account. I've gotten over my fit of jealousy," she confessed. "And I'm ready to hear all of the scandalous details. Since I'm not involved with anyone at the moment, I have to live vicariously through you, so come on and don't leave anything out."

"We're not seeing each other anymore." Terra went on to tell Lexi about how Mason lied, and that he wasn't in the real estate business but worked at the Black Door.

"You mean to tell me that he's one of those fine-ass servers behind those half masks who wear G-strings and fuck all night for a living. Damn!" she exclaimed. "I know without a fact that he's got some serious skills, because those servers are well hung and can lick the hell out of a pussy," she said, blowing a breath of hot air into the receiver.

"No," Terra nearly screamed, "he's not a server. He's the manager." She didn't want to picture her man parading around in a tiny piece of loincloth, showcasing his dick for a bunch of horny women.

"Well, if he's not one of the hired studs, then what's the problem?"

"The problem is that he's associated with the club, and if word got out that I was dating the manager of a sex club, all hell would break loose. First of all, the tabloids would have a field day, and secondly my parents would die of embarrassment, not to mention what a negative effect it would have on my career."

"Not to be mean, but what career? You're still auditioning for commercials."

Terra had been so distraught over breaking up with Mason that she hadn't told Lexi about catching Sage in a compromising position, and the movie contract he gave her to keep her mouth shut. "So, you see, I've got a lot to lose," she said, after filling Lexi in on the story.

"I can't believe Sage is a switch-hitter, but I should've known. He's just too fine and too fashionable to be straight. Why is it that most of the educated, good-looking, well-dressed men are gay?"

"I don't think Sage is gay-gay. It wasn't too long ago that he was trying to get into my panties. Remember?"

"Yeah, I remember. So, you think it's just a passing fad?"

"I don't know, maybe. But there's one thing I do know for sure, and that is he'd do anything to keep his father from finding out about his sexual experimentation."

"I'm sure he would. Mr. Hirschfield is so old school that he'd probably disown Sage if he knew his only son liked a little dick on the side. So what type of film are you going to do?" Lexi asked, switching topics. "When are you going to start shooting? This is exciting, I can't wait to come on set and see what goes on behind the scenes. Who knows? Maybe I'll meet a cute cameraman like Julia Roberts did, get married, and have twins." She chuckled.

Terra shook her head, even though Lexi couldn't see the gesture. "I swear, you are one man-hungry chick."

"It worked for *Pretty Woman*. Why can't it work for me?"

"Whatever," Terra said, dismissing Lexi's comment. "Anyway, the studio is still under construction, but in the meantime, we're deciding on the type of film we're going to make. Sage has been sending me all types of scripts so that we can narrow down the genre. I don't know if it should be a romantic comedy, a drama, or a suspense thriller."

"Wow, sounds like he's letting you in on some major decisions."

"You wouldn't believe how accommodating he's been. Before, it was like trying to pry information out of his mouth with a crowbar. Now he's so forthcoming, I really feel like we're partners."

"You're partners all right, partners in this hush-hush conspiracy to keep his father in the dark," Lexi said, setting the record straight.

"Frankly, I don't care what type of partnership it is, as long as Sage honors my contract and I star in his next two pictures." Just then, the doorman buzzed up on the house phone. "Lexi, I've got to run. The doorman is ringing, I'm sure there's another script waiting for me downstairs. I'll call you later in the week, and maybe we can get together for a drink."

"Sounds good. Talk to you later," Lexi said, and hung up.

Terra went to the lobby and picked up the package from her doorman. Upstairs, she opened the oversized envelope, but it wasn't a script. Inside was a one-hundred-dollar gift card from Borders, matches, a magnetic keycard, a menu, a postcard from a local artist, a transcript, and a letter. She spread the contents out on her cocktail table, looked at each one carefully again, and then read the letter.

> *Terra,*
>
> *I know, I'm probably the last person you want to hear from, but you're in my system, and I can't stop thinking about you. Though our time together was brief, it was memorable nonetheless, and I've gathered some mementos for you. The gift card from Borders is for your daily Chai fix (smile), and reminds me of the first time I laid eyes on your lovely face. The matches are from Pravda. The hotel key card is from our romantic night at the Gansevoort (when we made passionate love. REMEMBER??). The postcard is from the same artist who painted the picture that I bought you, and the menu is from our delicious lunch at Barolo. I've also included a copy of my transcript from med school, just in case you thought I was lying about that too.*
>
> *Terra, please give us another chance. I LOVE you with everything I am and everything I have!*
>
> *Mason*
>
> *P.S. I'll wait for your call, and if I don't hear from you … I'll understand.*

Terra read the letter over and over, until she had memorized every line. No one had ever written her a love letter before and she was deeply touched by the sentiment. The wording was perfect, even his handwriting was faultless, and she adored the fact that he had collected something from everywhere that they'd been together. And when she looked over his transcript, she realized that at least that part of his life was the truth, which made her feel a little better about the situation.

Maybe I'll call just to say thanks. I mean he did go through all of this trouble, she thought to herself.

Terra picked up the phone to call him, but someone was already on the other end of the phone. "Hello?"

"Hey, Terra. It's Sage. How are you today?" he asked, full of energy.

"I'm good. What's up?" she asked, a little annoyed that he had interrupted her flow.

"I found the perfect script! The story line is tight, and the lead role is dynamic. I'm having it messengered over to you this afternoon. Call me back as soon as you've read it over. This is it, Terra. I hope you're ready to become a star, because once this film comes out, you're going to be known not only as an heiress, but as an Oscar contender. This movie is going to do for you what *Monster's Ball* did for Halle, and what *Monster* did for Charlize. I can't wait to hear what you think. Talk to you later," he said, and hung up.

She was excited about the prospect of making an impact on Hollywood, but it also brought back the reality of how high profile her life would be if she was nominated for an Academy Award. She decided not to call Mason, because as long as he was affiliated with the Black Door, she couldn't afford to be affiliated with him. She knew it was a bit superficial, but she had her career to think about. There was a part of her that still loved him, but she would just have to put him out of her mind.

After receiving Mason's unexpected package and contemplating her future, Terra was emotionally drained and needed to rest her brain. She laid her head back on the sofa cushions and decided to take a nap while she waited for the script to arrive. Sleep came quickly, and before long she was dreaming in Technicolor.

She was at the Black Door, looking for Mason, but there was no one else in the club except for the two of them. Terra wasn't wearing a mask or a seductive outfit like before; this time, she wore her usual uniform—jeans and a white shirt with a cardigan wrapped around her shoulders. She roamed the darkened corridors, calling out his name, but he was nowhere to be found. Panic began to set in and her heart pounded with fear when she realized that she'd lost him.

"Looking for me?" he whispered in her ear from behind.

Terra spun around and threw herself into his arms. "Mason, I thought you left me."

"I'll never leave you," he said, kissing her neck.

His kisses tickled, and she felt a chill run up her spine, which made her pussy twitch. "I need for you to fuck me right now," she told him.

"But what about your reputation?"

She began unbuttoning her blouse. "I don't care about the tabloids. All I care about is having your dick inside of me," she said, taking off the cotton blouse and unsnapping the front hook of her bra.

Mason looked at her juicy titties and hard nipples and licked his lips. He took a step closer, but didn't touch her. "You want me to play with your titties and suck your nipples?"

"Yes," she panted with desire.

He wasn't wearing any clothes; he took his erect dick in his hand and pointed it toward her crotch. "And then you want me to unzip your jeans, and fuck your pussy until you cum?"

"Yes," she panted again. In anticipation, Terra quickly took off her jeans and panties. Now she was standing in front of him naked, ready for the fuck of her life.

"I would love to give you all of this beef," he said, rubbing his thick shaft up and down, "but I can't."

She reached for his cock, but he pulled away. "Why won't you fuck me?"

"Because you're an heiress, remember? And can't be associated with a lowlife like me," he said, still stroking his erect dick.

"You're not a lowlife. You're my man, and that's my dick." She dropped to her knees ready to suck him off, but again he moved away. She then lay back on the floor with her legs spread open. "Please, Mason, make love to me before I lose my mind," she pleaded.

He looked down at her luscious body and couldn't resist her any longer. He eased down on top of her and wedged himself between her thighs. He began rubbing the head of his dick against her clit, until she squirmed underneath him.

"Oh, Baby, that feels so good," she purred.

Mason parted her thick swollen outer lips and slipped the round head of his cock into her pinkness. He then began burrowing his rigid erection deep into her hungry pussy, plunging the length of his long pole back and forth and back and forth, with total abandon until he heard his sperm-filled balls slapping against her ass like cymbals clashing together in midair.

"Ooohhhh, Baabbby, I'mmmm cummming!" she screamed loudly.

Mason gave her a few more deliberate thrusts before releasing his army of life-giving sperm into her welcoming canal. "Damn . . . that was . . . good," he panted, and collapsed his tired body on top of hers.

Terra's body jerked and twitched in her sleep from the erotic dream, until she jolted herself awake. Her blouse was moist with perspiration, and her hands were wedged between her legs trying to quell her mounting desire. "God, I want that man!" she yelled into the room.

The dream made Terra realize how much she missed and wanted Mason. She sat up, reached for the phone, and dialed the first five digits of his cell number. She'd planned to tell him that she was willing to try their relationship again, and to hell with the tabloids. But as she dialed the sixth number, her sleepy lust-filled haze began to lift and she returned to her senses. She reluctantly hung up the phone, choosing her career over a life with the one man that she could never have.

29

THIS WAS the day that Sage had anticipated for months, the day his baby was born. Well, it really wasn't the birth of an actual child, but he felt like a proud papa nonetheless, since this was the evening that he was unveiling his precious studio to the industry. Pearl was back from sick leave, and had coordinated every single detail with the utmost care. She had hired a graphic designer to design the invitations, which resembled a motion picture screen with the details of the party written like movie credits. The oblong invitations were hand-delivered in silver metallic envelopes to New Yorkers, and sent by FedEx to the West Coast. The invitation list read like a Who's Who of the entertainment industry with media from all the top tier trade magazines and television shows, agents, managers, a sprinkling of stars, and a few venture capitalists to round out the group. Pearl also hired the best caterer in the city, and tonight's menu included grilled langostino, Maryland crab cakes, Blue Point oysters, lamb chops drizzled with a mint yogurt sauce, wild mushroom risotto, and white truffle ravioli. Money was no object, so in honor of the special occasion, she ordered cases upon cases of Cristal.

Sage arrived shortly after Pearl and did a walk-through to make sure everything was on point, which of course it was. His chest was so puffed up with pride that the buttons on his shirt nearly popped as he admired the state-of-the-art studio. To see the studio laid out on paper was one thing, but to see his vision come to life was awesome. There were two separate studios with high-tech cameras and lighting flown in from a German manufacturer. The third, smaller studio was set up as a screening room, with comfortable, oversized leather seats, a theater-sized screen, and an old-fashioned red and brass popcorn machine. The executive offices that lined the perimeter of the studio were just as impressive, with sleek furniture from Maurice Villency, custom-made blinds, and imported carpets from India.

He walked back into the main studio where the reception would take place and waited while Pearl gave the waiters their instructions for the evening.

"Make sure you distribute the hors d'oeuvres evenly around the room, so that everyone gets a taste of all of the delicious appetizers. Also, make sure that no one has an empty glass. There's plenty of champagne to go around, so make sure the flutes stay filled to the brim. Tonight's a celebration, and I want everyone to be in a festive mood. Thank you," she said, dismissing them before she made her way over to Sage.

"Pearl, everything is just perfect. I'm so glad you're back. I don't know what I would have done if I had to rely on those incompetent temps."

"Even if I would have had to coordinate everything from home, I would have never let a temp oversee something as important as this. I know it means a lot to you to show your father that you can stand on your own two feet. Sage, I've known you since you were a little boy, and I want to see you succeed as if you were my own son."

He gave Pearl a warm hug. "Thanks so much for your support."

"What's with the sappy sentiment?" Henry Hirschfield asked, walking into the studio.

Pearl turned toward her former boss and said, "I was just telling Sage how proud I am of him."

Henry looked around the studio and was pleased with what he saw; he'd never been on a soundstage before and was excited to be entering into a new industry. "I'm proud of you too, Son," he said, slapping Sage on the back. "Now what's on the agenda tonight, aside from eating and drinking?" he asked, as if he were still the CEO.

"Once everyone is here, Terra will make her grand entrance, and I'll introduce her as the star of Hirschfield Multimedia. We'll then go into the screening room for a clip of *Rage,* our first production, and afterward she and I will conduct a few interviews," Sage said, laying out the evening for his father.

"Sounds good, Son. I see you have everything under control. Call one of those waiters over," he said to Pearl. "I'd like to make a toast before everyone arrives." The waiter promptly came over with a tray of champagne and gave everyone a flute. "To Hirschfield Multimedia. May it be as successful as Hirschfield Publishing," he said, raising his glass.

"To Hirschfield Multimedia," Sage and Pearl chimed in.

Less than an hour later, the guests began to drift in, and before long the main studio was packed with some of the heaviest hitters in the entertainment world. With all the media hype surrounding the opening of an East Coast movie studio, everyone was anxious to see firsthand what the new facility had to offer. Sage spotted Roy across the room talking to two well-dressed men and made his way over.

"Gentlemen, I'd like to introduce you to Sage Hirschfield," Roy said, once Sage entered their circle.

"Sage, I invited two prospective clients to the party, so that they can see firsthand what the Roy Snyderman Agency can do. This is Trey Curtis, who owns a business uptown and is thinking about expanding. And this is his associate, Mason Anthony."

Sage shook their hands and couldn't help but notice how attractive they both were. He wondered if Roy had given them his special, personalized attention, in addition to designing floor plans. His dick began to come to life as he thought about how Roy sucked his balls and dick simultaneously. Sage hadn't had a blow job since Missy died. He had been calling her for days without an answer and decided to go by her apartment. That's when the doorman told him that she'd been killed by a bus. Sage was shocked into celibacy, but seeing Roy schmooze his prospective clients was bringing his libido back to life. "Nice to meet you two. Please have a look around. Roy is the best in town," he said, giving the architect a come-hither look.

Roy caught Sage's eye and wanted to suck him off right then and there, but he had to restrain himself, since the last time he went with his instincts, they got caught in the act. "Thanks, Sage. Working with you was indeed my pleasure," he said suggestively.

"We will look around. Thanks for extending the invitation," Trey said, and shook Sage's hand.

Mason didn't say a word. He was on pins and needles. He hadn't seen Terra since that night in her apartment, when he told her about his role at the Black Door. He thought for sure that she would call him after she read his heart-filled letter and saw the mementos that he had collected, but she didn't. Even though it had been a few months, he was still in love with her and was nervous about seeing her tonight. She had no idea that he would be at the studio opening and didn't know how she would react once she saw him. He didn't even know that he was going to the opening until the day before, when Trey invited him so that they could see Roy's work up close and personal. Mason mingled aimlessly through the crowd, looking for Terra, but she wasn't there.

When the room was at full capacity, the lights dimmed and Sage's voice boomed over the loudspeaker. "Ladies and gentlemen, may I please have your attention?" Once the chatter subsided, he continued. "Tonight, we have a special treat. In addition to christening our new studio, we're going to preview a clip from *Rage,* our upcoming feature. But first let me introduce you to the star of the film, Ms. Terra Benson." The crowd began to clap wildly as she made her way through the throng of people.

Mason's breath caught in his throat as he watched her breeze into the room. She was more beautiful than ever before. Her long, wavy hair was swept back into a tight bun. Her makeup was natural-looking, with just a hint of color on her cheeks and lips. Her ears and neck were adorned with flawless diamonds, and she wore a teal blue Vera Wang chiffon dress with tiers that floated in the air as she waltzed through the crowd. She looked every bit the star, and though she wasn't his woman any longer, he couldn't have been prouder. Mason was only a few feet away and wanted to stop her and say hello, but he didn't. This was clearly her night, and he wasn't about to ruin her moment.

"Now if everyone will join us in the screening room, we'll start the clip," Sage said once Terra had made her grand entrance.

Mason and Trey followed the masses and settled into two seats near the back of the room. The clip was short, but powerful. Terra's character was a pregnant prison inmate who'd been raped and beaten by a guard. Mason hardly recognized the woman on the screen as his gorgeous girlfriend, because her face was swollen and bruised beyond recognition. Her performance was compelling as she begged her court-appointed attorney—who could care less about his client—to have her transferred to another prison, since the warden had turned a blind eye to the injustices going on under his nose.

Once the clip was over, the screening room exploded with thunderous applause. Terra was brilliant, and everyone acknowledged her performance with cheers and more applause. She stood up and graciously took a bow, and then thanked Sage for his faith in her. She took a few questions from some of the entertainment reporters and then invited the group back into the main studio for more champagne and dancing.

"Wow, she's extremely talented," Trey said, taking two flutes of champagne from a passing waiter once they were back in the main studio.

"And beautiful too," Mason said, watching Terra mingle across the room. After twenty minutes of admiring how she charmed the press and chatted up fellow actors, Mason couldn't take it any longer. "Look, man, I've got to go. Seeing her continue with her life without me is pure torture. I'll talk to you later," he told Trey.

"Wait a second, let me finish my drink," Trey said, turning the glass up to his lips. "I'll go with you."

Trey and Mason made their way to the exit, but before they could leave, Terra looked up and spotted them. She mouthed for Mason to wait, and then quickly finished her conversation with her agent.

"That was a great performance," he said once she was standing in front of him.

"Thank you." She touched his arm. "And thanks for the package. I wanted to call you, but—"

"There's no need to explain. I understand," he said, cutting her off. "But just so you know, I have the money now to continue with med school, so I'll only be working at the club part-time." Since

Mason didn't have to give his life savings to Missy, he had decided to finish his education.

A wide grin spread across Terra's face. "Excuse us please," she told Trey as she grabbed Mason's hand, led him into one of the executive offices, and shut the door. She didn't bother to turn on the lights. She just reached up, grabbed him around the neck, and planted a wet juicy kiss on his lips. "I've missed you so much," she said when they came up for air.

He kissed her forehead. "And I've missed you too, but are you sure a relationship with me is what you want? Even though I'm back in med school, I'm still working at the Black Door, and I wouldn't want my involvement with the club to cause any problems for you," he said, pinning her with a serious look.

"Mason, I was wrong to let you go because of your job, and I wanted to call you a hundred times, but to be honest I was concerned about the press. Now that I've had some time to think things over, I've come to realize that no matter how hard I try to keep my personal life private, reporters are always going to pry. It's their job. I can't continue to live my life afraid of what's going to come out in the press. So to answer your question"——she stared deep into his eyes——"yes, I'm sure I want a relationship with you. I've been thinking about what you said that night at my apartment. You're right, a love as strong as ours doesn't come around every day. And if it comes out that you work at the Black Door, then so be it. After all, it's not like you're selling drugs on the street or operating an illegal brothel." She took a step closer to him. "Besides, I know you're the one for me . . ."

"And how do you know that?"

"Because you've been in my dreams every night," she said, giving him a kiss on the lips.

Her words were music to his ears, and he thanked his lucky

stars for a second chance. "So, Ms. Benson, tell me about these dreams of yours," he said, nuzzling his nose into her neck.

She pressed herself against his crotch and began to grind until she felt his dick respond. Then she whispered in his ear, "They're quite nasty."

"How nasty?" he asked, grinding her back.

"First of all, we're both naked," she said, unzipping the side zipper on her dress and slipping out of the couture gown. She then took off her strapless bra and thong.

Mason took in her luscious titties, small waist, and slim hips and licked his full lips. "Are you sure? This is a special night, and I wouldn't want to ruin it for you."

"You'll ruin it if you don't make love to me." She walked over to the door and locked it. "Don't worry; nobody can get in now," she said, crossing the room and lying on the sofa.

Mason tore off his suit and followed her to the couch. He made sweet love to her, until they both were crying from the tenderness. "I love you, Terra."

"I love you, Mason, and don't ever forget it," Terra said, giving him a deep French kiss.

While they were in the office declaring their love for each other, Trey was having another glass of champagne. He was eyeing all the beautiful women at the party dressed in sexy designer dresses and draped in exquisite diamonds, no doubt on loan from Harry and Jacob. Trey loved people-watching, and was enjoying the sights when his eye caught a familiar face. He hadn't seen her in months, and now she was coming in his direction. He wanted to turn and walk the other way, but she clearly had him in view. *What is she doing here?* he wondered.

30

"FANCY SEEING you here."

Trey gave her a polite smile, but didn't really feel like striking up a conversation. "Small world isn't it?" he asked, knowing that trying to avoid her now was futile.

"I haven't seen you since that rigorous interview a few months ago." Lexi grinned. She had wanted to chat him up when she joined the Black Door, but he was acting so professional during the interview that she couldn't get her flirt on. But now that they were in a party environment, she hoped that his guard was down. "You want to dance?"

"No thanks, I'm not much of a dancer," he said, taking a sip of his champagne.

Lexi's eyes roamed the full length of his body. He was dressed in a coal black suit, white shirt, and silver tie. She couldn't help but notice how his broad shoulders filled out the suit jacket. He was one fine man, and she wanted to get to know him better. *I bet he's a good lay,* she thought. "Oh, I find that hard to believe. I bet you're good at everything." She winked suggestively.

Trey pretended not to pick up on her blatant flirtation. She was a beautiful woman; her skin was the color of caramel, and her short brown hair was streaked with blond highlights. She wore a snug black evening gown that hugged her body in all the right places. And her diamond necklace sparkled brightly underneath the glow of the lights. Yes, she was indeed beautiful, but he had gotten into deep trouble before for fucking a client, and wasn't about to go down that road again. "Thanks for the compliment." He finished the last of his drink and said, "It was nice seeing you again, but I really have to be going."

She took a pen and a piece of paper out of her purse, wrote down her number, and handed it to him. "Call me sometime; I would love to teach you how to 'dance,'" she said, putting emphasis on the verb.

Trey quickly turned around and walked away, before she caught him up in her web of seduction. As he was making his escape, he ran smack into another unwanted face.

"Hi, Trey." She smiled warmly.

Suddenly his heart began to race, and his underarms began to perspire, but he quickly composed himself, leaned in, and kissed her on the cheek. "How have you been?" He did a once-over, and she looked better than the last time he'd seen her.

"Well as can be expected under the circumstances," she said with a sad tone in her voice.

He nodded because he understood exactly what she meant. The circumstances that she was referring to were dismal at best, and he preferred not to think about the past, but one look into her eyes and all the memories—good and bad—came flooding back. He remembered the first time they had met and the immediate attraction that they felt for each other. He thought that he was over her, but standing in her presence brought back the feelings that he had suppressed for so long. "Do you know Sage Hirschfield?" he asked, changing the subject, trying to get his mind off the heat building in his crotch.

"I don't know him personally. Yates Gilcrest handles all of Hirschfield Multimedia contracts, and Bob, one of the managing partners, invited me tonight, since I'm in town for a few days," Ariel said.

"So how's Washington treating you?" Ariel had moved to Washington after she had married his father.

"Well, it's not New York, but I'm managing." She smiled slightly.

"And how's my dad doing? I've been meaning to call him, but the club keeps me busy," he said, trying to avert his eyes from hers, but he couldn't help but stare into her gorgeous face, a face he couldn't forget.

"Actually, that's one of the reasons why I'm in town. We have to talk," she said, lowering her voice and looking around to make sure that no one was within earshot. "I was going to stop by the club, but now I don't have to," she said, fidgeting with her evening bag.

Trey immediately thought back to the last time they were at the Black Door together. It was the night when he fucked her so hard that his mask fell off and she saw his face, and realized that she'd been having an affair with her future stepson. "What's the matter?" he asked, sensing trouble.

"I think Preston is starting to remember." When his father found out about their deception, he'd had a mild stroke and lost his short-term memory. Trey, Michele (his girlfriend and Preston's assistant), and Ariel decided to keep the truth from him as long as possible. Preston was in the middle of being nominated as a Supreme Court Justice, and they wanted to spare him the devastating deception.

Trey didn't know what to say. He knew that one day he would

have to own up to what he'd done, but he didn't think it would be this soon. "What makes you think he's regained his memory?"

"Because he's been treating me extremely coldly, and he doesn't have much to say. Normally, he rushes home and tells me about his day, but lately he's been staying out until one and two in the morning. I think he's trying to avoid me."

"Maybe he's just busy. After all he is a justice now," Trey said, trying to calm her fears as well as his own.

"But what if that's not the case and he's remembered everything? Then what? What are we going to do?" she asked with panic in her voice and tears welling up in her eyes.

Trey didn't have any answers. He was just as nervous as she was. He'd committed the ultimate act of betrayal; now it was time to face the music, only he didn't like the tune that was playing. "I don't know, Ariel. I just don't know."

extracts reading groups
competitions books new
discounts extracts extracts
competitions extracts reading groups discounts events
books new events reading groups
events books extracts
new extracts discounts reading groups
titles reading groups
interviews events new
events extracts extracts interviews books
discounts events new books
new books events interviews new books extracts
events new extracts
discounts extracts discounts books

www.panmacmillan.com

extracts events reading groups books
competitions books extracts new